C000053941

About the Author

Dreena Collins was born in Jersey, Channel Islands, where she now works in education; she has a background in English teaching and Special Educational Needs.

Previous publications include poetry featured in *Mslexia* magazine and *Interchange* periodical, as well as a short story in the *Eyelands* International Collection, in 2018. She has been shortlisted and longlisted in several writing competitions, including the Wells Festival of Literature Short Story Competition, and The Bridport Prize.

Things that Dreena loves include comfortable shoes, island holidays, spicy food, irreverence, and her family.

She dislikes intolerance (and Jaffa Cakes).

http://dreenawriting.co.uk
facebook.com/dreenawriting

Dreena Collins

the blue hour
Short stories vol. one

First published in the UK in 2018

ISBN: 978-1-9993735-0-4

Cover design by Dreena Collins

Front cover quote courtesy of Mandy Snook, Education Advisor and Copywriter.

Back cover quote courtesy of Julie Brominicks, Freelance Landscape Writer:
https://juliebrominicks.wordpress.com

Silhouette art modified from images appearing at:
www.clipartqueen.com

Contents

Little Gems and Riches

Arthur walked past me, carrying a cup of tea, flickering, tremoring – the mug ready to turn as a shooting star. He made it to the sideboard and placed it down (too heavily) on a coaster beside me.

'Humph,' he said. He did not look at me.

He turned back to make the long journey to the kitchen again. He shuffled in his pyjama bottoms, feet poking out from open slippers, nails and toes both peeling like baby snail shells. This was the indignity of having to move.

By the time he had found his way back to me, he had left a trail of tea splatters on the carpet and he was red – crimson - in the face.

'There we are, then,' he said, with his gruff affection. He waved his hand as if to pat me on the leg. 'There we are.'

He took a sip of his tea. I could see it was too strong, and it looked to me as if it was made in the cup, not the pot. It put me off glancing at my own. I didn't want him to think me ungrateful. I knew what it had taken him to make it.

'It's nice to see you,' he stated, 'Nice when you come around. You know.'

He took a deep swig. It must have been too hot. Would have burnt his mouth, I was sure.

We sat for a little while in silence. I could feel the weight of his body on the couch, almost pressed against me, shifting the cushions and warming me up. He was quite close; I liked it. I could even smell the tea on his breath.

After a little while, he shuffled himself upright. He rocked his body back and forth, long arms pressed down hard into the sofa cushions - an octogenarian chimpanzee - until he finally swung into an upright position. Once upright he stood for a moment. He swayed. Then he grabbed the remote control from the occasional table and jabbed at it, to turn on the television; I knew this was for my benefit though once it sprung to life it was so quiet, I could barely hear it.

Then he was off again: an unsteady potter.

'Must get the dinner on,' I heard him mutter.

It was only half past four.

I watched him come in and out of the kitchen, back and forth half a dozen times, until on the dining table he placed two knives, two forks. A pair of coasters. Salt and pepper. Two glasses. A miniature world in binary.

'I'm making sausages,' he said, as he looked down onto the table. He sounded terse, but I knew him of old. He was proud of this little display, of this menu.

He glanced over, and I gave him a full beam of a smile. He knew I loved sausages.

'I hope there's peas,' I thought – but I didn't dare say it aloud.

He caterpillared his feet back into the kitchen again. I could almost see the static on the carpet. I tried not to look, stared at the television before me and enjoyed the clatter of the pans, the smell of the cold tea beside me.

When he was a young man, Arthur had been both delightful, and terrifying. He was terse but affectionate; steadfastly loyal and reliable - but I didn't think I could recall a time when he had cooked for me. He had developed his domesticity and skills it seemed. It seemed strange now, to see him grow so much - yet shrink so far. Strange to both wonder in awe and sorrow. The world is mercurial in that way.

I watched him each time he came out of the kitchen door but tried not to stare.

After a comfortable little while, the telephone rang. He fought with the handset and its miniature buttons, not made for old and clumsy fingers.

'Yes?' he shouted into the phone.

I chuckled inwardly. He was angry with the caller before he even knew who they were – but I knew that in truth he was angry at himself, his awkwardness, ineptness.

'Just making dinner,' he said, and then, after a pause '...what do you mean?'

He turned around to look at the clock.

'I don't care,' he stated, curtly, 'We were hungry.'

He listened further and then he was scowling.

'We... It doesn't matter. Yes. Yes... I have to go. The potatoes are on the boil,'

He started to move back towards the phone's stand, picking up his pace as he did, as much as he could, at least.

'What! Why?' he spat out, 'Ok, do what you like.'

He slammed the phone into its holder, had to jab at it several times to bring it home.

'Edward's coming around,' he muttered as he walked towards the kitchen. 'He's invited himself to dinner. Silly sod.'

It would be wonderful to see Edward again: but Arthur would not want to hear this.

He wandered back into the kitchen to tend to the food while I watched the screen, where professional chefs seemed to be cooking for professional critics in expensive but odd, modern surroundings. In the living room, I could not help but notice the thick dust on the table where the television stood – occasional lines of clarity on the glass table-top poked through it, where the remote was dropped and picked up again, daily - writing in the sand.

He came back out with another mug of tea for me. He held it high in the air, arm outstretched like a gauntlet, a prize before him. Ostentatious. When he reached the sideboard beside me he realised there was already a mug there, and seemed surprised. He managed to pick up the cup of ageing tea with his left hand, and swapped them, dowsing his right pyjama leg as he did so. He glanced down.

'Oh!' he cried, softly, 'I must get dressed!'

And he was off again, shuffling towards the bedroom, through a door on the other side of the dining room.

I stood and stretched my legs while he was gone.

On the mantlepiece were a series of pictures; most were familiar, had been there years. Shots of Edward when he was little, one of Arthur in his fishing gear, galoshes to his knees - the picture now weathered and dark and hard to make out. There was a formal one of me and him, together, a picture that I had always hated and which I had not known he had framed. I smiled.

Between the pictures there were little gems and riches – an old lottery ticket, a toy from a Christmas cracker, a pair of dice, a scrap of torn paper with a phone number on: no name.

He came back out from the bedroom again, but he was still not dressed. Instead he was carrying out a small bundle of washing and a newspaper.

'Right then,' he said confidently, 'Gravy!'

He put the washing down at the empty end of the dining table and attempted to balance the newspaper on top. It slowly toppled to the floor. He tried to catch it but waved his arms awkwardly around him, his fingers lacing the air, ham-fisted, maladroit. He caught the edge of the paper and it continued to fall, but now even further away. He started to bend, to retrieve it from the floor, but his bend had not reached to his waist when he thought better of this and he straightened up. Instead, he kicked the paper with his flaky foot until it was hidden beneath the table. Then he walked back into the kitchen.

Tears brimmed in my eyes.

The doorbell rang, persistently. A few seconds later he came out of the kitchen, seemingly a little panicked.

'Sit at the table!' he cried.

I did as instructed. He watched me settle before he walked to the door.

The front door entered straight into the living room and so I observed him attempt to peer through the spyhole and then fumble with the chain. He opened the door, and Edward stood there, waiting, a look of benign affection on his face, with just a hint of impatience at its edges.

'Hi, dad,' he said, 'What are we having?'

'What?' Arthur said, 'I'm busy.'

'Let me in, dad. It's cold out here.'

'Should have worn a coat,' Arthur said, as he moved to the side, to let Edward pass.

'Hello, hello,' he said, and then, 'It's dark in here, dad. Haven't you opened the curtains today?'

Edward began to move around the space, gently and efficiently, tidying cushions, opening curtains and windows, turning off the television, moving the washing into the utility area, and then collecting the mugs and a couple of side plates that littered the surfaces like debris. He smiled the whole time. Said nothing. Made no judgement.

'Can I help with tea?' he asked.

Arthur was implacable. He wanted him gone. He remained stood by the front door, hands balled as fists by his side.

'Can I smell sausages? Are they burning?'

This was enough to set Arthur in motion, back into the kitchen.

Edward sat in the chair opposite me, saying nothing, but still softly smiling.

Arthur came back out, carrying a jug of gravy, filled high, almost brimming over. Edward jumped up and took it from him.

'Don't sit there!' Arthur yelled. 'I'm sitting there.'

'Ok, Ok dad. I'll move.'

He made as if to move around to the other side of the table.

'You can't sit over there, either,' Arthur stated.

'Why?' Edward asked, eyes a little narrower.

Arthur stared at him, fronted him out. His cheeks grew pinker.

'Your mum is sitting there,' he stated.

'Mum?' Edward said. He looked at me, he looked through me, perplexed.

'Yes,' Arthur replied quickly, 'She likes sausages. You can't have any. I haven't got enough.'

11

A pause.

'Mum's not here, dad,' Edward replied, quietly.

I stayed still and watched them, these two men in my life. Edward young, confident, lithe: unsure how to deal with his now ageing father. Arthur still held his respect and was still the head of this family. But at the same time, he was an image, a faded photograph, of his former self. This was the privilege of being allowed to grow old. The privilege and the shame.

'Yes, she is.' Arthur stated. 'She is.'

Both men stared at me, at my place, at my self, at my absence.

'No,' Edward said, after a beat, 'No, dad.' And then, 'She's away, dad. Remember? She's gone.'

I knew what he was trying to do. But at the same time, I wondered what the point of this was. Why shake it off, bring him back – why take him away from me again?

Sometimes it's more important to be happy, than it is to be right.

'See, dad...'

And slowly, gradually and mildly, he walked over to the chair where I sat, and pulled it out, tipped it up, moved it around in the air. I moved away. I started to move away.

'No!' Arthur cried. Despair.

'See?' Edward said, so carefully, so softly.

And then he sat down on it, to join his father for dinner, and in a flicker, a tremor - on a shooting star - I left them again.

The Test

The door was gaping open; it was an escape route. It was a trap. Across the threshold, a pile of cellophane was scattered idly in a mound; discarded like a cheap carrier bag.

Yet that cellophane was precious.

Because there, right before him, was a pile of exam papers – naked and exposed.

Their exam papers. His exam paper.

It was probably foolish to stand still, staring, but Dan was held fast in a trance. Swiftly, through his mind came a rush of thoughts; justifications; guilt. He had an overwhelming urge to enter the room. But what if someone caught him? And really, was it right?

Screw them - after the year he'd had. After the time he'd had. Screw them. After Katy.

He glanced up and down the corridor rapidly, and stepped into the room.

This was where they had put him for the exam; all the adults together, they had said, so they didn't have to sit with the kids in the main hall. It was an old classroom, kitted out with cheap, motivational posters. They clearly hadn't finished setting up, although there wasn't long to go until the exam started, and a few sheets of scrappy work lay on the floor - rotting leaves at the base of an old, wooden shelving unit.

Dan moved hastily towards the papers and grabbed the top one. What the hell. He flicked through; Section A: to be expected; an extract to read, non-fiction, the usual – a newspaper article and a task designed for teenagers from the 1970s. 'Write a letter…' (What teenagers write letters these days? Reads newspapers?) Anyway, easy enough.

Section B: now this was what he needed; the creative writing section. When else in his life was he going to be required to make up a story and write the whole thing in 60 minutes, flat? In preparation, he had even considered writing three different stories and learning them off by heart, and then regurgitating whichever one seemed most appropriate.

But who was he kidding? He was much too lazy for that.

Three questions; choose one.

1) Describe the last holiday you went on. (Ha!)
2) 'The Girl in the Red Dress': write a story that has this as the title.
3) Write a story that ends with the words, 'And that was the last time I saw her.'

Hands trembling, Dan put down the paper, straightened the pile, stepped out the room and back into the corridor. No one was there; he hadn't been seen. A wave of exhilaration and relief rushed over him – settled as a pumping sensation in his face. He shook himself all over, vigorously, a wet dog, and then strode back down the corridor towards the common room, hoping not to bump into anyone he knew.

The common room was heaving with anxious students, talking too loudly. A small cluster of them were hanging around by the vending machine near the doorway as he came in: the girl with the bad hair extensions from his Philosophy class; her mate from in his English lessons, the one with the Latin quote tattooed up the inside of her arm (Emma? Emily?). They were OK, but he had no intention of talking right now; when they went to say hello he barged past them, eyes trained on the coffee machine in the back corner.

He had to weave through tables, a slalom, avoiding eye contact. He wasn't one of them, anyway; he didn't even fit in with the handful of older ones about the place. They were 'real' students. He was just a tourist, here for the ride, hoping it would drop him off at the right stop, taking him vaguely in the right direction.

At the coffee machine was another short queue, but thankfully no one he recognised was in it. He stood behind a young lad with dangerously low-slung trousers. He wondered again how he had ended up in this College, and whether it was realistic that he would come out of it, equipped and able for Uni. He thought not. It had been almost fifteen years since he left school, and he couldn't say it had been an easy return to education. And it was either perfect timing, or dreadful timing, depending on your point of view. After what had happened. Katy.

He glanced up, wondering where he would sit, to mull over the paper without interruption. He caught the eye of Bill, one of the guys on his course, a good bloke. Bill had a stick, seemed better some days than others. A wincing scenario popped into his head from a few months ago: Bill was having a bad day, and had tried to rush to the toilet, suddenly. He obviously hadn't made it: when he staccatoed back in, sometime later, he had a very small, but clear, wet patch emblazoned his crotch. It was almost, but not quite, symmetrical.

A broken moth.

A group of three girls had started mewling together about it in a disgusting way. Bill had sat there and ignored them, but Dan noticed his hand shook when he took notes. Ill health, or shame? It stung, either way.

At the end of the lesson, Dan made a bee-line for the tutor to talk to her about it, asked why she hadn't said or done something, what she planned to do to sort it out. He was angry; he raged. She was extraordinarily myopic, in response.

'Well, maybe you should say something to him – he's your friend,' she said.

Dan had stared at her, incredulous. It wasn't Bill who needed talking to. It was the girls.

Katy would never have behaved like that, if she had ever gone to College. He was sure of it.

He shook his head, to shake her image out of his line of sight and return it to the back of his mind, back where it grew just a little, occupied just a little more space, each day. A rhododendron taking roots: the most beautiful flower in the garden, but invasive, spreading. Taking control.

The last time I saw her.

Eventually, he was at the front of the queue. He had his money ready and selected his drink. The cup dropped, and the drink dispensed, slowly. The boy next in line seemed to take this as a cue to make small talk. He was babbling away –dialogue like an annoying cat, slinking against his legs, repeatedly, unwanted. Talking about how the Student Council had campaigned for a new machine. What the hell? Painstakingly, Dan slowly lifted his head and stared hard at him, unspeaking; the boy soon dried up.

He barged between the overcrowded tables, holding his drink high, a chalice. He found a table piled with junk in the back corner. Not only did the kids think they were too good to put their rubbish in the bin, but they also thought they were too good to sit at a table covered with someone else's rubbish, it seemed. Dan piled most of it up onto a tray, and then put this on the empty chair next to his, daring anyone to misread the signs, daring anyone to disturb him.

He got out his black, leather notebook from his bag and retrieved a pen from his pocket. 'The Girl in the Red Dress'. Could he really write a story, about her? Could he? Irritatingly, he noticed that the table was sticky, just as he started to focus in on the idea. The two thoughts collided, and a sense of Katy's warm, jammy hand, in his, tingled his palm briefly.

She did have a red dress. A knee length one, with a tiny, delicate white pattern of flowers on it, and three buttons that were just for show running down the front. It was the colour of raspberries. Is that red? But the dress wasn't particularly sentimental, and he didn't have any special story attached to it, apart from, tenuously, the obvious one, the big one.

And he couldn't write about that, could he?

Dan could feel the pumping blood in his face again as the sound of her voice crept out from where he trapped it, as he tried to squash it and flatten it under the weight his impending exams, one very imminent impending exam, and the fact he had to be back in that exam room in five minutes. He needed to push it back again. No time for dwelling on her laugh, or her one-dimpled cheek, or her cloud-soft hair. Or the fact that it all came crashing down, scorching and blistering him to the very bones. To his bones.

And that was the last time I saw her.

Could he do it? Should he? It was the most obvious thing to write about. No excuse for writer's block there. His English tutor had always told them to write from their own experience. (No zombies, werewolves or mafia allowed, she said.) Dan had a flair, she said. He must do the advanced paper she said, try to get a top grade. He had allowed her to decide for him. 'Dan, I know you can do it,' she said.

The coffee was going cold; he gulped it in a few swigs and rammed his book and pen back in his bag. On the way out of the room he nodded at Bill, as he rocked himself into the upright position, pushing down, hard, onto the arms of his chair. He nodded at Emily (or was it Emma?) and her mate, he even nodded at the boy who had tried to talk to him in the queue. What the hell. At least, he thought it was the same boy – or maybe he was just nodding at random strangers now.

He strode down the corridor quickly – annoyed with himself - how had he managed to make himself late? What the hell? Flexing his hand again as he went, both wanting to shake off and yet preserve the feeling of her delicate fingers in his.

The room was pretty full by the time he got there, but they hadn't started yet. Dump your bag at the back, grab your pen and find your name. If he had the nerve, this one was going to be easy, in its way. The last time I saw her.

Dan took some deep breaths; tried to ignore his throbbing face. On his desk already was an answer booklet for him to record his responses. He started to fill in his details on the front, and then glanced around the room, to check protocol. No one else was writing anything so he figured he'd best stop. No point in drawing attention to himself.

The invigilator was handing out question papers, gently sliding one onto each desk, having told them not to open them yet. Dan's paper was balancing precariously on the edge of his table, like it may fall, yet he had a weird sense that were he to touch it, to move it to safety, this might give him away. He watched it. A Ming vase, ready to crash.

Now she was back at the front of the room, gently and quickly relaying rules and instructions about mobile phones and black ink and staying to the end and it was all so soft and quick, like a ball of tangled wool slowly unravelling from her mouth. He tuned her out, waiting for the cue to start, tapping his pen on the desk. Trying to prepare himself for the writing task. He did need this grade, after all. No point throwing the year away. Trying to think about Katy without the crushing tidal wave of emotion that came with these memories, trying to think about the last time he saw her, and yet trying to continue to breathe.

And finally: 'You may begin.'

He turned to the back of the paper straight away. There it was. 'And that was the last time I saw her.' No point putting it off. He labelled his answer booklet: Section B, 4. He started to scribble a notional plan, for the sake of it, like he had been told to, when an older woman he didn't recognise put her hand up suddenly and said, much too loudly:

'Excuse me, we shouldn't be doing this paper.'

The invigilator flew over and tried to shush her, but a little tremor shook around the room, nonetheless. What did she mean? Shouldn't be doing it? A tiny prick of panic grew in Dan and he started writing quicker, more furiously. Did they know? But how? Or maybe this woman had been given English but was meant to be doing something else… maths maybe. That could be it? Or she could be in the wrong exam. Yes. Dan didn't think he'd seen her before, anyway.

He continued writing, although behind him, he could hear rustling and whispering, and he knew something was wrong. He tried to continue. And that was the last time I saw her. The last time. It was.

Then the invigilator was tapping him on the shoulder and he felt an overwhelming urge to cry. What the hell? He looked up, and saw that she had another exam paper in her hand.

'I'm sorry, you have to swap papers,' she whispered. 'I'm sorry. You have got the wrong paper.'

'I'm fine,' Dan growled, and looked back down. 'I'm doing English; I'm fine. This is my paper.'

He held onto it, protectively, and pretended to get back to writing.

'No, love,' she said, calmly. 'This is a Foundation paper. I'm sorry, you need the Higher paper. See?'

She pointed to a black, block H on the front of her paper. Dan flicked to the front of his, to see an F there, mocking him. F for Foundation. F for Failure.

Damn stupid tutor, getting him to try for a higher grade.

In disbelief, he briefly let go of the paper and dropped his hands, and his pen, to the table. The invigilator saw this as defeat and swiftly swapped over the two papers.

'There love, all's well now. We'll give you an extra five minutes to make up for it. We'll make a note for the exam board. Sorry, love.'

And then she was on to the next person in his row.

So that was it. He'd let himself think about it and there had been no need. He'd faced the horror for no reason. The last time I saw her. For nothing.

It was too much. A vortex of pain and anger engulfed him, and he wanted to knock over this chair and scream; he wanted to tip his desk and bang out of the room and tell this College, and tell the world what he thought of them all. And forget it all, and screw it all, and who did they think they were, anyway? And who was he kidding, thinking he'd be able to get into Uni, anyway?

Clearly, he was only ever destined to be dealt the crap hand.

Why had he expected anything different? After this year; after...

He pushed his chair back, jaggedly.

The girl to the left of him looked over and gave him a shy smile, then turned back to her work, concentrating so hard he could hear her breath. She had tied her hair back into a sensible pony tail, had a little row of identical black pens laid out on her table, and an orange highlighter in her hand that she was using to mark sections of the text. He could see she had numbered the paragraphs. She had slipped her sandals off under the desk and sat cross legged, leaning hunched over, right up close to the paper. She was trying so hard.

A little cough, someone clearing their throat, broke his thoughts, and he looked around to see the invigilator staring at him, eyebrows raised. She probably thought he was trying to cheat. The irony made him smile. He snorted with laughter. She shook her head at him.

So, still with his chair pushed back, set to leave, he picked up the new exam paper for a glance. The last time. His face was really throbbing now, almost rhythmically, and a whooshing of blood pounded in his ears.

Ok. Think. Maybe, dear God, there were some of the same questions on this paper – he steeled himself, forced himself to check. Section A was different, but the same formula of course. 'Write a letter to your town council...' (Seriously?). Then came Section B:

Three questions; choose one:

1) Describe a room you know well.
2) 'The Man with the Black Car.' Write a story that has this as the title.
3) You walk through an unlocked door, into a room you are not allowed to enter. Write a story about what happens next.

Dan stifled another laugh, stretched his fingers out, scraped his chair closer to his desk, and shook his head, gently.

So. Write from your own experience. No zombies, no werewolves, no mafia. He took a deep breath, picked up his pen. He ignored the blood hammering in his cheeks, in his ears, the noise, the ache, the weeds, the memories.

He started to write:

The door was gaping open; it was an escape route. It was a trap. Across the threshold, a pile of cellophane was scattered idly in a mound; discarded like a cheap carrier bag.

Yet that cellophane was precious.

Because there, right before me, was a pile of exam papers – naked and exposed.

Our exam papers. My exam paper.

Where the Water and the Shingle Meet

Marion leant forward and pinched a bundle of cotton wool between her index finger and thumb, so that her right hand formed an 'OK' symbol.

She stared at it, and its lie, before lifting a bottle of cleanser with her left and dowsing the wool, drenching it with liquid. She swept it across her face: cool, a relief. Her cheeks turned pink.

This might be her last performance.

Lowering herself backwards in the chair, she noticed that the ribs of its back bowed slightly as they took her weight. Still light, still slight - yes - but Marion was nonetheless bigger than in her youth. There was no denying it.

The chair, at least, did not lie.

In front of her, the image of an ageing woman obscured her true self in the mirror. Who was this person? She tried to see through her, but the many light-bulbs surrounding the glass illuminated every etch on her skin. Harsh. Brash. Marion forced herself to look. Forced, as a slowly turning corkscrew of discomfort twined in her stomach.

She sighed.

She leant forward to turn on the radio. It would be frowned upon, she knew, to have it playing, but she needed the distraction. Still, she'd be able to hear the call, the action. She was an excellent multitasker, if nothing else. The radio helped to move her on, bring her back into the room and away from reminiscence.

Beside the radio was a colossal bunch of flowers. A gift from her son. Happy flowers: gerberas punctuated by a few small, but exquisite, sunflowers. Appreciate the present, she told herself.

She glanced over at the beautiful dress, her costume, draped and ready to wear. Bejewelled. Gold. She felt her old self again when dressed in it. It hung there, patiently for her, as it had so many times before.

It was the canary in the coal mine. And it was still vivid, still here.

'I'm not dead yet,' Marion said, aloud, solidly.

She had done this countless times, and there was only a small audience tonight, but her nerves were palpable. She was one step closer to retirement, to moving on, to this change of identity, of name, of persona. More than a step. A leap. Then who would she be?

Carefully, she blotted her face with a tissue, ready for her make-up. She went back to work.

She picked up a small, grey tube of primer and begun. Primer. For painting the walls of a house, a home. These days she needed it, to smooth over the cracks.

'All OK?'

Sam stuck his head around the door all of a sudden, causing her to jump. He did not enter the room.

'Got everything you need?' he asked, kindly, with just head and upper torso leaning in: only this much of him daring to enter her space.

She gave him a smile - a reassuring one, she hoped.

'Of course,' she said.

He loitered a little in the doorway.

'Knock 'em dead!' he said, unconvincingly.

'Um… you too?' she chuckled, without laughing, 'Oh, and good luck, I guess!' she added.

'Yeah,' he said, and winked, before closing the door behind him.

Lovely Sam.

Marion turned back, to face the mirror, stared hard at herself then picked up a glass jar of liquid foundation. She rolled it between her hands, back and forth, felt its cool hardness against thin, dry palms. She had to force herself to stop, the rhythmic movement was a child's swing; a lullaby.

She took the lid from the jar and poured a dollop of thick liquid onto the back of her hand. She opened the top right-hand drawer, to find a small sponge, which she used to dab at the foundation and apply it to her face.

She spread it delicately, across her skin, returning again and again to the same spots, spreading it out from her nose, to the periphery of her face; layering it up over and over until it airbrushed away some of the lines, the creases, the wrinkles. The lessons. It was smooth. It was dense. It was reassuring.

Her reverie was snapped by the sound of Alan opening the door, tersely. He came striding into the room without speaking, and the fissure of light and noise where the door remained swinging open, in its portal, broke her spell.

It took him only four steps to reach her dressing table.

He placed a crystal-cut glass of gin and tonic heavily down onto the surface. It swilled up, almost to the edge, back and forth, as it settled. Two small, already melting cubes of ice danced atop the liquid, as life rafts.

'There,' he said, gruffly.

He dropped his hands by the side of his body. An awkward, shy, little boy, in an awkward, angry, old man's body.

'Oh!' Marion said, in genuine surprise.

'Well?' he asked.

'Thanks?' she replied, tentatively.

'OK,' he said, and paused, before turning on his heel, and walking away. He shut the door behind him, loudly, closing off the outside sounds.

This was the way he spoke to her now, and these were the things that he did. They were tentatively dancing at the tide, in the space where the water and the shingle meet, on the shore. On the edge. Are we in, or are we out?

There was a time when she had loved him, of course, and he her. And now this. They were forced together, in this mockery of real life, in this art, artifice. They were together most days, squeezed into this tiny space of discomfort. Was it worth it?

No.

'Only one more night,' she whispered to herself, eyes closed.

When she opened them, her glance settled on the drink, its two pathetic, dwindling ice cubes still tottering atop, but slowly dropping down. Sinking.

She took her concealer and dabbed at her face. Dabbed at the dark patches beneath her eyes, dabbed even at the two stubborn, interloping spots of acne that had found their way to her chin (extraordinary!). Then she found her powder, loose, like talc, and covered herself in its veil. Finally, she swept on blusher, into the hollows of her cheek.

Next, she began on her eyes.

There had been a time, not so long ago it seemed, when the implicit was explicit. When all was said between them, and the subject would not lay beneath the surface or under the skin as some hint, some itch. Rather, it was shouted, yelled, cried - kissed. Alan was a sniper with his insults. Quick to draw, sharp. Marion was slower, and reticent. But clever. They had damaged each other.

And now, in essence, she was alone.

She leant back into the bowed arch of the chair and looked at her reflection. She should probably wear more on her eyes, but she was reluctant, and tired. Instead, she took a sip from her drink. It was lukewarm, and strong. It was good.

Marion took her favourite hairbrush from the second drawer. Her hair was already half pinned in place, from earlier: it just needed a few pieces releasing, some last touches, a fluff up in places, a smooth down in others. A spray.

Alan used to love her hair. He would brush it for her. He would stand behind her, at this very chair, sometimes, and rhythmically move the brush through it. She would close her eyes and not bother about the bright array of bulbs, the harsh image in the mirror. The wrinkles. Incredible now, to think that a man so gruff, cold, could have been so tender.

'Stop it; stop it!' she spat, and shook her head, 'Focus, woman!'

She needed to think about tonight. And herself.

Marion stood for a moment and thought over her words. Lines prepared and used so many times, they were worn down and etched into her somehow now, they had become a part of her. She didn't need to worry. She knew what to say.

She stepped towards the dress, slipped off her towelling dressing gown, ready to revel in the process of dressing herself in this second skin. Just as she did so, and stood cold, exposed in her underwear, Alan burst through the door again.

'Five minutes!' he called, loudly - too loudly - and then, 'Oh,' he said.

At least he had the decency to look embarrassed.

Marion stared at the floor.

'Five minutes,' he said, 'It's your call.'

She continued to stare at the floor, didn't want to look at him, until she heard him shut the door, quietly this time.

'Stupid sod,' she muttered.

She was cutting it fine, with time though. She had not realised. Annoyingly, his call was useful. She picked up the dress and slipped it over her head, carefully. She should have done her hair afterwards, of course, but she loved the showmanship, the happy surprise to see herself, now completely herself, when she finished getting ready and took a final look in the mirror.

Marion turned to take in her reflection. She felt relieved to see this reflection again.

One more night. This was her curtain call.

Her phone buzzed. Sam.

'Hello?' she asked, concerned.

'Hi, mum,' Sam said, 'Sorry, sorry, sorry – you are probably getting ready?'

'What is it?' she said, 'What's the matter?'

'No, nothing, don't worry; I just meant to say, I mean, I forgot to remind you that we are out for breakfast tomorrow. I won't see you later. Are we still on for it?'

Marion smiled to herself. Her son, her one accomplishment. She prayed to God he would understand her reasoning when she broke it to him tomorrow – told him that she was leaving.

'Aren't you supposed to be on a date?' she laughed.

'She's in the loo,' and then, more quietly, 'seems nice, and doesn't have two heads, so that's something.'

'Oh, sounds promising!' she smiled, 'Yes, breakfast tomorrow. I assume not too early, seeing as you are out.'

'No…. and dad's not being… you know, too much, like *dad,* is he?'

'Everything's fine,' she said, 'and it's an important evening for him… But listen, I really have to go.'

She was leaving this lie.

'Bye! Love you,' she said quickly, and ended the call.

'Taxi's here!' Alan yelled, from the foot of the stairs.

Marion picked up her handbag from the wardrobe, and glanced down at the small suitcase resting there, partially obscured by her clothes, and she took one last look in the mirror.

Then she turned and walked from the room, and down the stairs - to meet her husband, and hold his hand, and laugh at his jokes, and play the part of the dutiful wife. She would stand on the shore and put a toe back into the water, where it would be warm, and familiar. But transient.

Her final act of kindness.

Steak and Something Pie

Dad said that if he was raising a 'cissy boy', he may as well reap the benefits. By which he meant so long as I was interested in cooking, he'd keep on coercing me into making his tea.

Mum said cooking wasn't for cissies; that was a long of crap; that I should do whatever made me happy. But she said it quietly and urgently into my ear, a spray of water from a hose that stopped as soon as it started. Shut off.

I said nothing.

I took a bag of carrots from the fridge and started peeling. By my feet sat Petra, her long nose resting on my Vans while her tail swept the floor, slowly, gently. Old now, her sight was failing in direct proportion to her scent increasing.

'Hey girl,' I said, 'pie for dinner.'

One ear twisted around at the word 'pie' but she didn't even have the energy to lift her head. In years gone by, she would have ricocheted around the room at those sounds - 'pie' or 'dinner'. 'Beach'; 'biscuit'; 'ball' would all have the same effect. I sighed, noting the long gloop of saliva that fell from her mouth onto my shoe.

The irony was, I wasn't even going to be eating this. When I had reminded dad that I was out this evening, watching Kyle in his am-dram production, he had reeled:

'Am! Dram! Ooh. Am. Dram,' his pointy face bent forward close to mine, too close to mine, sharp and glistening as a blade, 'your gay boy antics don't change my plans. I'm in a relationship too. A relationship with pie.'

He laughed at his own joke, muttered 'relationship with pie' under his breath several times. Laughed some more.

I am not in a relationship.

Mum wasn't even going to be eating this either. She was out with Aunty Anne on their bi-annual Chinese and wine night.

I finished chopping the carrots, reached down under the counter into the vegetable rack for the onions, trying hard not to disturb the dog. More saliva congealed around her and my heart gave a little wobble. I grabbed a clean tea towel and gently mopped it up; gave the top of her head a tussle between the ears when I finished. She hardly stirred.

Into my mind drifted a memory, like a seed on the air. It was planted, though I didn't want to think on it. It grew.

Mum coming back, a giggling thing with sparkles in her eyes. Happy. Tipsy. Drunk, even. Unusual for her. It wasn't late; eleven maybe? Dad in his chair. A junk yard of empty cans by his side. Didn't look up. Glowering. Eyebrows set. I came out from the kitchen at the sound of the front door shutting. Felt the clash of their two auras, saw the tension as the two tones, two moods, met each other. Somewhere between the side table and the front door, Dad's belligerence won out. A wave of black. The shouting started. Mum gave in. She had the fear in her eyes. But dad didn't stop. Then the tussle. I intervened; it was broken up quickly, thank God. I didn't say much.

In fact, I didn't say anything.

When they were quiet I went into the kitchen and put the kettle on. I came back, just minutes later, and they were wrapped tightly into each other, limbs a mess, over and under each other like a ball of elastic bands. And dad was snoring, already, snoring, and mum was looking at me, staring and beseeching - lost eyes in a tangle of body parts.

I shook my head. Put the onions on one side. Needed to get to the fridge for the meat, and any other suitable left-overs I found, to throw in. Veggies. Not quite sure what sort of pie this was going to end up being.

'Sorry, old girl.' I said to Petra.

When she raised her head, I noticed that her left eye was weeping again. I picked up the tea towel without thinking, gently wiped away the gunk. Dabbed at her jaw again before moving upright. The poor thing.

When I got back to my place with the meat, I grabbed a new chopping board and got to work; started mulling over Uni applications again. I was caught between a rock and hard place. A hard parent. I knew what I wanted to do - Art - and where I wanted to go. Mrs James said I had a good shot at it, too. But I hadn't even said anything to dad yet, well, because of the obvious. Because I knew how he'd react. He'd already made it clear how he felt about Art. Even picking it as an A Level had sent him into a tailspin. He'd raged about the influence of my 'batty boy' friends - none of whom were actually doing Art, of course. I'd only gotten away with it because I'd 'balanced it' with 'proper subjects' - business and physics. And now I'd ended up with the most bizarre grade profile and subject combination you could think of.

I'd broached the subject with mum after parents' evening a couple of weeks ago. Dad hadn't been there. Mum was twinkling with pride after meeting Mrs James, who had laid it on pretty thick.

'I want to go to Art College, mum.' I said, quickly and quietly, while we drove home in the car.

For a long time, she didn't speak.

Then she said, 'I'll talk to your father.'

And that was it. But it was three weeks' ago and as far as I knew, she hadn't yet raised it with him. And I hadn't said anything, of course. This morning, we had all had breakfast together in silence. At one point, I had almost convinced myself to speak up. I held my breath and stared at Dad, trying to judge his mood. He spotted me, and his face puffed a little, his whole body swelled, slightly but perceptibly:

'What are you looking it?' he shot out.

'Nothing.' I said.

I shut my eyes closed, tight, at the memory, at the wince of it.

'I'm not even gay you know, Pets.' I said.

I moved over to the other side of the kitchen and bent to get a saucepan out of the cupboard, lit the gas on the hob.

Petra stirred and stood up gingerly. Her legs clearly stiff, she seemed in pain, and an almost imperceptible whimper came from deep inside her. I noticed a tiny trickle of urine escape down her back legs onto the floor. I grabbed the tea towel, wiped it clean, rubbed her head, washed my hands again.

'For God's sake, don't ever let dad see you doing that,' I muttered.

I knew it was a matter of weeks, days probably, but couldn't bear to say goodbye yet. I knew it was selfish; of course, I knew it.

As the meat gently browned, I made up a gravy and grabbed the ready-made pastry from the fridge. Dad would want homemade, out of principle, but I couldn't be bothered, and he wouldn't know the difference anyway. I rolled it out, lined the greased dish with the pastry carefully, pricked the bottom, stuck a sheet of parchment paper in and then some dried split-peas for weight, to stop it puffing up too much. I put it in, to bake it for a few minutes.

'No soggy bottoms for me Petra, only you.' I muttered.

I turned my attention back to the saucepan and seasoned the meat, added the carrots, lowered the heat. I'd found a bowl of mixed up veg, threw that in for good measure.

Just as I started working on the gravy again, Petra gave a little yelp. I turned to see a little pebble of a poo sitting in the middle of the kitchen floor. I grabbed the tea towel, pinched her offering in the middle and carefully carried it out into the downstairs toilet where I dropped it in. I grabbed a bottle of some sort of cleaning spray and pointed it vaguely in the area where the accident had happened, sprayed and wiped with my trusty tea towel.

'I won't say anything, Pets, you can count on me.'

I sat down next to her for just a moment and leant into her tough, scrawny body. A hot, beefy scent emitted from her; she was brittle and worn, but her heartbeat sounded steadfast and strong through her chest. She was still alive. I had the tea towel in my hand, so gave her poorly eye one last gentle pad, being careful not to use the same section.

'Back to work, girl,' I said.

The meat was starting to catch as I poured the liquid in. It wasn't going to be my best effort. Still, the sharp and rich scent of red wine had filled the kitchen with comfort. I allowed the gravy to bubble up and thicken in the pan, and cook through for a few minutes. The second-hand vegetables started to disintegrate and crumble into the liquid. As they did so, I rolled out his pastry lid on the flour, and on a whim, I cut out some pastry leaves to decorate the crust.

I retrieved the pie case from the oven, where it had sat a little too long. The pastry had contracted away from the edge a little. I'd have to make sure the top was large enough to compensate.

Then I turned off the saucepan to let the contents cool slightly before adding them to the pastry case. I glanced around the room at the clutter and mess I had made. I'd never been a tidy chef; flour, pastry and gravy spluttered one counter top like a happy memory. I surveyed the scene and then went back over to the other side to scoop the carrot gratings into the bin.

I moved to the pie dish and gently poured the contents of the pan onto the pastry. There was a little left over that I'd give to Petra later, so I took her clean dog bowl from the drying rack and tipped the leftovers in, to cool. I took the prepared pastry sheet and laid it across the top of the pie, delicately, a baby's blanket, until it covered the whole thing and draped the sides, then pressed the edges down, making a deep lip around the sides before neatly slicing away the excess.

Gently, I cut four slices into the top of the pie to release the excess steam, and it burst through the first hole, hot breath into cold air. I took the leaves I had cut and placed them gently onto the top, to embellish the pie, so that it looked that it contained much more love and care than it actually did.

'Now we really should glaze it, girl,' I said, '... but I know we don't have any eggs...' I tapered off.

I paused and looked around the room again.

I picked up the tea towel and gave Petra's mouth one last wipe. A teardrop of spittle had been hanging from her lips, as gel. I caught it in the cloth.

I stopped. Thought. Then walked over to the pie and gently unfolded the tea towel over it. I lay it flat across the pastry top and patted down, all over. I flipped the towel and did the same, then spotted a globule of something, greyish, yellowish sitting on the pie crust. I rubbed it in, clockwise, gingerly, carefully, so as not to break the surface. I unfolded it again and screwed the towel into a fist, and spotted a distinctively brown stain right in the middle of it, so smeared all the juices and fluids carefully, delicately across every millimetre.

I looked down at my masterpiece and smiled softly to myself.

'It's better than nothing,' I said to Petra.

Something Old, Something New

The sun was opening her rays, and she was persistent. She pulled Claire up to the surface, on a hook, on a thread. Rising.

She could feel her body fill and swell with restlessness as the light strengthened – her mind fill and spark with thoughts and concerns - until she was there; in the hotel room. Awake. She broke the surface and there was no going back: puppet arms, kicking legs and a mouth, yawning and gulping as a fish.

5.30 a.m.

She lifted one heavy leg out of bed and dropped it to the floor, then slowly made her way across the room to the kettle. A mild hangover came into view just as the remnants of sleep disappeared. Next to the tray, with its tea bags, instant coffee, was an open bottle of red wine, two thirds – no, three quarters - drunk. It had an ugly smell: guilt, bitterness.

Tea made, Claire shuffled back to bed, fluffed her pillows, switched on the bedside lamp.

Your wedding should be the happiest day of your life.

She was entering today with eyes puffy from alcohol and lack of sleep, and more than this, she was experiencing a sensory assault: mild nausea, itchy skin, her body temperature too hot and the air too dry, stale. Even if she could shake this off, she would be mildly cranky and fuzzy-headed all day, no doubt. Just when she really needed to keep it together.

She had been agitated for days, sleeping poorly and feeling anxious. And now, here, the cumulation of all of this meant that her body was so overwhelmed that her brain could not think straight at all, could not sort and catalogue her thoughts as needed, could not prioritise what was urgent, and what could wait.

Her mind was a cage full of bingo balls. No. A Hadron Collider. Her mind was a large Hadron Collider with pipes, beams, circling and travelling in opposite directions. To unsettle; to spin; to split. And she was searching, scouring, looking at details that were smaller than atoms. Looking at details. Smaller and smaller.

Claire closed her eyes.

'Get it together... Get it together,' she whispered, hoarsely.

She tried a few deep breaths, in and out, then suddenly remembered her wash bag. In it, she had beta-blockers, vitamins. She had taken Vitamin C for years, and had been to the Doctor just this week for the beta-blockers. An elevated pulse, he had said.

She took the two little tablets together with a swig of tea, happy to give them a try.

Something old, something new.

It was only 5.50am by then, and she promised herself she would not begin getting ready until at least 7, as the ceremony wasn't until 10am. She had a taxi booked for 9.30, so she'd have to string out the dressing and prepping for some time as it was. Alone: she would do it alone, having declined all offers of company and support this morning. This had been the right decision.

At 6am on the dot, at the time specified in the information pack, she called for room service – a full English, and coffee ('strong, please,') on the side. She turned on the television while she waited, left it mumbling in the background as she inspected her nails and spray tan to see how it had held out, overnight. The whole experience was surreal - sitting in a strange bed, watching programmes she would never usually see, hungover, waiting for food she would not usually have, on the morning of the wedding. The marriage.

Breakfast arrived a full twenty minutes later, and she asked the young lady to leave the tray directly on the bed. She looked slightly alarmed by this request – her eyes gave her away – but nonetheless politely did so.

Claire took the tray and balanced it on a pillow across her lap, her body propped up against the headboard. She bolted the food and felt all the better for it – even though the fried egg was cold and hard, and the baked beans mushy. She ate it all, and between the food, caffeine and tablets she was improved in herself. She did feel better, yes. She could do this. This was her day.

She carefully lifted the tray to carry it to the dresser, for now, and on the way back to bed she pulled the curtains apart to illuminate the room.

She sat on the edge of the bed and looked out of the window, onto the roads converging, the few cars traversing the junction outside the hotel. Her thoughts had started to settle into an orderly fashion, finally. Again, they fell to him.

When she thought of Adam, as she so often did, the love she felt had a giggly excitement, a buoyancy that lifted her. Even now, she felt a little flicker in her stomach at the sound of his voice, or a text message, a glimpse of him. Even now.

Yet the aftershocks were there. The terror and horror of when she had found out about Emily and what he had done, what he was doing; the deception. The deceit. He had taken her heart, her swollen, ripe, bursting heart and shocked it to stone. Shattered it. Pulverised it, even. She had never imagined him capable of this; trustingly, foolishly, it had never occurred to her he could, or would, act in this way. And now, she knew she would never be the same person again, the girl she had been. Trusting. Naive.

Gullible.

And so, he had morphed, in her eyes, into someone else – into two people. He was both the Adam she had known and loved, and yet this other Adam: this liar, this cheat. This bastard. He was both of these people. Popping in and out of focus. And it was impossible to resolve this neatly. For one to erase the other.

Because both versions of him were true.

It made her feel sick, dizzy again, to think of it.

'Get it together.'

Over the last couple of months, she had been able to bring forward in focus his older self. The man she knew. She had dropped new Adam into the background. He was still there, still lurking, still in view on occasion – but old Adam was in the foreground and he overshadowed him and blocked him out - usually.

This would have to do. This would have to be good enough. Because she had no other way to do this, to cope. And she needed to cope – what other choice was there? To lose her way, her mind?

He was relieved, it was clear, that she had stopped haranguing him, that she appeared to have moved on from it. He had been desperate when it blew up, when it came out: the one time she had ever seen him tearful. But now, she thought, not sorry enough – not quite sorry enough. He had moved on, too. But his moving on was real, not a coping strategy. He seemed almost to have forgotten it all, already. So, she wondered what the future would bring: would he really make a steadfast, loyal husband?

A family man?

She looked down to notice she had been picking at her thumb nail: rubbing the crimson polish until the gel had started to lift from the nailbed, and peel away. And she had not noticed when she had started to cry. It happened often these days, with such ease. It was bizarre, the distance, the gap between her and others, herself and her own feelings. She was still somewhat numb: was cut off, like a house cat, looking out on the world through a window.

She took a few steps to the bedside cabinet and pulled a wodge of tissues from the box by the side of the bed, then sat back down, heavily.

Something blue.

Was she doing the right thing today? Maybe not. But it was all she could think of to do. And this was why it was better to be alone today. Not to face the sympathetic faces, or the pep talks, or the judgement, even. The judgement. She wasn't the one who had cheated. Who had lied, exaggerated, hidden and lied, repeatedly, relentlessly for so many months. Only he did this.

'Get it together… Get it together,' she muttered, slowly rocking, slowly.

She stood up, walked over to the dressing table and poured the remains of the wine bottle into a mug. She downed it in three gulps.

She walked back to the bed and shook out the sheets, brushed the cover down, made the bed, tidied the pillows. She took the tray and placed it in the hallway, outside her room. She turned off the bedside lamp, now redundant. She surveyed the room.

It was almost 7am.

Claire gathered her make-up bag and opened it, laying out all the instruments she needed on the dressing table. She was meticulous with her arrangement of it all. She did not wear much make-up as a rule, and Adam seemed to like it that way. But this was such a special occasion, and she had so much time, she knew she would be layering it carefully and subtly on her skin this morning. And this was for her, not him. A visor.

As she surveyed it, for a moment she felt the old panic and fear, then took the plastic bag that contained her hair-drier and brushes, spray, clips. She emptied each out onto the bed in an orderly row, checking that she had all she needed. This order, this pattern was reassuring to her. It made sense.

She took her perfume, and her necklace and bracelet, sparkling and shocking, and placed them on the other side of the bed, to be the last piece of the puzzle before she walked out the door.

Together.

Finally, she went to the wardrobe and found her dress, where she had hung it so tenderly the night before. It was a long, ivory gown but not heavy or thick. Satin, its bias cut clung to her and felt cool and comfortable. She had lost almost a stone in the last few months and would not have had the confidence to wear such a dress before. But now, she wanted to wow everyone – including Adam – and yet, perversely, at the same time, she cared much less what people thought than she had, previously. Screw them.

So, they could judge her if they liked, they could critique, but she was passed caring.

The room was getting brighter, and at her feet, her own shadow swiftly drowned in the harsh sunlight - disappeared.

It seemed she was really going to do this.

As she slipped off her pyjamas, and pulled down her hair, ready to shower, she tried to picture Adam's face when he saw her. Arriving at the church; the look in his eyes. His face when her heard her voice, as she spoke to object to his wedding, to his life ahead with Emily - his mistake.

She hoped she could stay calm.

It had been real. It had. It had been whole. It had been theirs. If he could not see that, she really had been left with no choice.

She was not the other woman - something borrowed. This was hers. And she would take it back.

Pillow Back

Paul was aching for a beer.

He had been sat on the sofa for what felt like a couple of hours, although the clock maintained it was just 25 minutes.

Sat on the sofa, now stiff, immobile, moulded into the seat.

It was a 'pillow back' sofa, Sara had told him, and the whole piece was constructed from a mound of soft cushions, curving around him, cocooning him. Cooing to him to stay where he was. But he couldn't stay there forever.

It was odd. He didn't really know how he felt; couldn't put his finger on it. Happy, of course, yes, he felt happy. And relieved, undoubtedly relieved. He had been building up to that conversation for so long - dreading it. So, he was definitely happily-relieved it was over and had gone well. So calmly and quickly.

It was odd though, how well she had taken it. That was a bit - unsettling.

For the past six months, maybe more, she had been desperate, she had sensed it, he guessed. Clinging to him. Hands everywhere. Her. Everywhere. And her response, when he told her, was therefore startling in its composure.

But it was good, though; of course, that was a good thing.

Eventually, he psyched himself up to put one hand down on the sofa, to begin to extricate himself from the cushions. Then he paused, shook his head. That motion alone would have caused Sara to ask him where he was going.

'I'll get it!' she would cry, if he'd told her he wanted a beer.

He grimaced. God, that pissed him off. Used to piss him off. So needy. No need to worry about that any more. Hah!

He tried again. That bloody sofa. It was irritating, the way his hand sunk into it, the way he was squished into it and had to put so much effort into getting up. It was dense, needed tense muscles and force, just to get out of it. Quite frankly, it made him feel old.

On the way to the kitchen, he spotted a half-drunk mug of tea, sitting on the table. He paused. A little blob of orange-brown skin was forming in the centre. It was out of place; Sara never would have had that. He didn't think he'd ever seen a cold cup of tea on a piece of furniture in this house. She was ubiquitous: a tidying, preening whirlwind in the house. Spinning through the place, grabbing things as she went. His things, he supposed. She wouldn't have left them there in the first place.

Well, she could go to hell. This was his space now.

He left the tea to fester on the table, walked past it into the kitchen, felt weirdly proud.

Cold beer in hand, he had a moment where he had a strange mental blank. He couldn't for the life of him remember where the bottle opener was. Irritated, he opened and shut drawer after drawer, then remembered it was stuck to the fridge (the bloody fridge he had just opened) by a magnet.

He leant against the counter and reflected.

She had come home from work, and he was waiting for her. Often, she was home before him. Especially lately, when he had been in no rush to get back to the house. But today he had been packed up and ready to get out of work on the dot of five. He had driven, figuring it was worth the cost of the parking for the day, for the confidence in knowing he'd be there early, and she'd be the one on the back foot.

When he heard her key in the lock, he had jumped up. He was stood in the middle of the living room when she came in. She was taken aback, and paused, one hand clutching a bag of shopping and the other held slightly up, in the air, still holding her bunch of keys.

She was wearing that ridiculous scarf again. It immediately filled him with rage, making the next part all too easy.

'I need to talk to you,' he said.

She nodded. Slowly placed the shopping on the floor. It settled in defeat against her leg, and a bag of frozen peas toppled out, half way out, towards the ground.

'OK,' she said.

And that was it, that was how it went. No tears. Just some nodding. Some *I understand*s, some *I know*s, and even an *I agree*.

And then she went. Just like that. She said it was probably easier if she spent the night at Jayne's: she grabbed some clothes, a bottle of wine, and took all his anticipation, his fear of hysteria out the door with her.

And now that bag of shopping was still sat on the kitchen counter, waiting to be put away. He grabbed the peas and put them in the freezer. Simple. Then yoghurt. Straight into the fridge. Like a boss. But then next there was an aubergine. What the hell are do you do with that? Fridge? Cupboard? He settled on 'cupboard'. Gave up on the whole thing once he realised the next object out the bag was going to be some sort of bunch of herbs.

Well, it was 6.15, and the night was young. He should do something, call Phil. Get him to come out. He hadn't seen him in ages. They could grab a bite to eat, get some drinks. He and Phil went back a long way; he had even confided in him a little about his plan, about Sara.

'So, what is it, though, is there someone else? Or have you just, you know, gone off her?'

'I don't know how to explain it. She's just… annoying,' Paul had said, 'she's so over-the-top nice all the time. And predictable. It grates on me. She fusses around me all the time. Drives me mad.'

'Like what?'

'I don't know,' Paul said, 'take last night. We were on our way out, she was all excited. She spent hours getting ready. We'd planned it for ages. Carluccios. We had this voucher. Nice, right?

I had this vague headache; nothing too bad but just… there. You know? And as we are going out the door, she asks me if I'm ok. And I tell her I'm fine, just a bit of a headache.

And she pauses. And I know straight away what will happen. I regret saying it. The minute I've said it, I think: I know where this is headed. So predictable.

She goes, 'Do you want to stay in?' All… earnest. Standing too close to me.

It's bloody infuriating. Like we were going to stay in! After all that. And it just made me feel guilty. Sometimes I think she even does it on purpose, so she can, I don't know… be the better person or something.'

Phil was standing there, staring at his drink; head down, frowning slightly.

'I don't really know what to say to that, mate,' he said, quietly.

'I know, right?' Paul chuckled.

Well, that was over a month ago now, and he hadn't seen him since. It would be good to catch up, and not to have to start from the beginning with the whole story. He already knew. How she had been so full on. Fingers around him, gripping, clutching as to a pole, hanging on to him.

He fished his phone out of his pocket, and realised he had three percent battery. How did that happen? His eyes darted about the place to look for a charger. Now, where did they keep the chargers?

Jeez, what was the matter with his memory today?

Anyway, no rush. He could do whatever he wanted, now. He could go out, stay in, do things at his own pace. He grabbed another beer. Wondered back into the living room. Settled into the 'pillow back'. It was squidgy. It was marshmallow. He hated to admit it, but it felt good.

Sara's voice popped into his head.

'You don't appreciate me, Paul. We both know that,' she'd said to him.

Didn't appreciate her? Didn't appreciate being pecked and fussed over, more like. He shook his head. Took a large swig, spilt a splat of beer onto his chest. The fabric stuck to his skin, thick, sticky, uncomfortable. It would have to stay that way.

If he was going out, he'd have to iron that shirt anyway, so he'd get changed then. It had been ages since he'd ironed, and the thought of it was enough to put him off going out at all. He'd have to hunt for the ironing board, grapple with it, to put it up... Maybe he'd just leave it, call Phil tomorrow.

He'd stay in. That's right. Stay in. He'd watch some trashy TV, or a movie even. He never got to just sit and pick a film these days. So. He'd watch anything he wanted, something he'd *appreciate.* He chuckled.

Now, where was the remote control?

Elevated

What she knew was this. It was about a year, only a year, since she had gone to the Doctor. She had a shake with a jitter in her bones as he spoke to her. She didn't want to; could not stop. He was talking, and she was focusing so hard on smiling and nodding and steadying that she forgot to listen. And shaking so much she forgot how to be calm. Be calm.

'So really, what I am saying is - unless you strongly object – I'd like to sign you off work.'

'No,' she said.

Because in spite of it all, she did. She did object. And she was. She was strong.

And so much stronger now.

She reminded herself of this journey because although she could not say she still loved, missed or yearned for Pete, she could not help but think of him, occasionally. The thoughts and memories crept in, unexpected, sometimes. Gave her a jolt, and then scuttled - a little black beetle in her brain. She tried to shake them out and off, but it did not always work. The feeling of shame that came with them was the worst. The shame of it all.

Even now, as she sat scraping wallpaper from the kitchen wall, they skittered in for no reason and gave her a shudder.

She leant over and turned the music up a little louder, focused her ears on Jimi Hendrix, and her thoughts on cleaning up this wall.

— — —

As he locked the door of his flat he had that dull grey feeling that he'd forgotten something, the same feeling that he got each and every time he left home. Annoyed with himself, but barely attempting to resist the urge, he patted his pockets, shook the door to check it was locked, looked in his bag - again - to verify his file, his iPad, his work fob. It was all in place. Of course.

He strode towards the lift, vaguely disappointed in himself, his irritation compounded by the sound of some nasty, dirty, electric guitar that drifted up the stairwell towards him.

— — —

She sat in the coffee shop, reflecting on the morning she had just had. Work was so slow, so boring, and yet, somehow, she was still doing a bad job. It was quite remarkable, really. In downsizing, downscaling, she'd become strangely dull in her thoughts, and now this morning had found herself in the bizarre position of having someone with less experience, less age, less qualified, explain to her what she needed to do for the third time - clearly thinking her an idiot. For some reason she just couldn't focus, and the instructions drifted around her: a series of unconnected words, dots. A dandelion clock.

She needed to get out of that place. She needed to stretch herself. Fingers crossed the meeting she had on Thursday might lead to something.

The beetle stirred and tried to lift his head, but she moved quickly to ensure he didn't wake. She took her headphones out of her bag and popped them in her ears, and on a whim, she sprayed her wrists with some Chanel - and then she grabbed her things and made her way to the door, and back to work.

— — —

He held the door of the cafe ajar for a woman going past and then tentatively walked in. The cafe smelt of dark, bitter coffee and heavy perfume, a familiar scent. He was scouting the place out really, having been once or twice before. His meeting on Thursday was going to be held here, and he wanted to get the lay of the land beforehand.

He queued for coffee and took the place in with fresh eyes. It looked expensively shabby and painfully up-to-date. Pretentious, really. He spotted a couple of out of the way seats that would suit a lone coffee drinker. The place was full of young couples, laughing and leaning in to one another wearing scarves and beards.

He didn't mind sitting alone, been doing it for years. God knows how long it had been since he'd sat drinking coffee with a woman. His friends thought this odd, thought he must get bored or lonely, or miss the sex perhaps. But the truth was that most of the time he didn't mind. Most of the time he was perfectly happy, and he liked the liberty to do what he wanted, to eat his weird meals, to sleep in if he liked, or to get up at five, to clean the kitchen for the third time - all his anti-social habits and peculiarities. They only seemed weird when held up against someone else's behaviour - and he liked the lack of mirror. He'd quite like some female company sometimes but she'd have to be, frankly, amazing. Pretty much perfect to make it worth the effort.

And in his experience, most people were far from perfect.

— — —

She lugged her bags into the flat, scraping the wall and getting under her own feet. Through the stairwell she could smell someone else's dinner, appetizing and accomplished. She was tired, clammy, and irritated. She dragged the bags inside and dumped them on the sofa. She had spent too much, but already knew that she felt uncomfortable in everything she'd bought. Except the shoes, perhaps.

Now she had to think about dinner, which always made her feel incompetent. A child. An imposter. She didn't deserve a new career. She couldn't even make her own pasta sauce, for good sake.

She leant forward into the kitchen cupboard to reach for a jar of sauce, and the little black beetle skittered across her hand, across her skin, into her thoughts.

'You're useless,' it told her.

She slammed the cupboard door shut. Opened the fridge for the wine.

— — —

He had meant to go shopping for new clothes today, ready for Thursday. Instead he'd found himself in the market, buying ginger. He was irritated with himself and the predictability of his avoidance strategies. He always cooked when he was stressed, and always tried, without fail, to convince himself that it was OK because it was productive.

'But you can't wear a bloody tagine to a job interview,' he muttered aloud.

Besides which, it wasn't as if he was practical in any other way. He couldn't do any DIY, wouldn't know where to start under a car bonnet. The wallpaper in his kitchen had been peeling for months now, lifted by the steam from all the cooking, he supposed.

From downstairs, he could hear the faint thud of some slow and heavy seventies rock. He found himself humming along, as he reached across the counter for the bottle of wine.

— — —

Thursday had come along all too quickly, and she had arrived at the café for the meeting a hollowed-out shell of herself, an ant-farm of scurrying nerves and beetles. She was cold, yet sweating, and uncomfortable in the stupid clothes she had bought. She was cursing herself for not exchanging the cardigan for a bigger size. She was cold, yet sweating. Cold yet sweating. Who does that?

She pushed on a door that was meant to be pulled, and let herself into the café. She glanced around the place, took in the model-esque barista, and an awkward-looking man in a baggy suit, before spotting her table, her fate.

— — —

Sitting in the café, he felt like a fraud, an old man, yet a baby. All around him were men with suits that were shorter and tighter than his. They had waistcoats, tie-pins, cufflinks and tattoos. He had none of these things, and sorely regretted not attempting to shop for a second time.

He picked up his macchiato and dropped a blob of milk-froth flotsam, straight into the middle of his tie.

— — —

The meeting had not gone very well, she feared. They asked the simplest of questions, so simple that she found herself searching for the trick, the hidden meaning, the right answer. She was a pinball, bouncing from one thing to another, giving half-finished sentences and jumping from one topic to the next. She had been manic, really, her eyes flitting around the room and taking it all in but making no sense of anything. A tiny coffee cup; mismatched wooden furniture; a stained tie.

And then at the end, just as they were wrapping up, the younger woman in the jumpsuit (a jumpsuit?) had asked if she had any questions for them. She suddenly found herself becoming urgent and serious, leaning forward to give an intense speech about how much she wanted the role and how much she had to give. It was a bizarre battle cry.

She had looked down at her own hands, strangely pink, to see them wringing a serviette into pieces.

— — —

He had left too abruptly, he knew, but he also knew that he had blown it. So, he just wanted out. He had stood up quickly and shook the guy's hand, firmly. He picked up his bag and paced towards the door, noticing a small pile of ripped paper on the floor as he went, a spot of which was now still stuck to his shoe. Of course.

At least he had tried. He had gone into the water, and had felt the fear of drowning, but he had survived. Nothing much could be worse than this, going forward.

He had gone straight to the corner shop nearby, bought the ingredients for Arrabbiata. He was going to binge on carbs and Rioja. He'd probably eat it in his pants.

This was one of those few times when he wished he'd met that perfect woman he sometimes dreamed about.

As he approached the building he was scowling, hot, bothered.

— — —

She stepped inside the lift, clutching a bag containing a frozen pizza and six small beers. She wouldn't be stripping wallpaper tonight, she would be stripping straight into pyjamas. Perhaps shrining would call her mum.

She pressed the button for the third floor. Felt herself sigh so deeply that her shoulders dropped, heavily, below their usual position. The lift doors started to close just as she glimpsed a harassed looking man, not an unattractive man, reaching forward to halt the elevator.

— — —

And then the lift doors opened.

Guarded

While she was talking, the space around her dropped away until only she was left. Left bare, enhanced, in sharp relief. She was all I could see. She was all there was. Everything.

Beyond her opening sentences, I took in no words. All I knew was that she was going to be with him, and I was losing her.

'It's exciting, right?' She said, grinning.

'Um, yeah, yeah, I… I guess.' I managed.

Her face dropped.

'Don't you think it's a good idea?'

Did I think it was a good idea? No, I did not. From what I'd seen, Tom was an utter sod. Manipulative, selfish, a hanger on. She'd even hinted at worse. He undermined her, he let her down, and still she always seemed to make excuses for him. She deserved more, and she would be unhappy with him, taken advantage of. I could give her what she deserved. I could. But she didn't see it.

She held me in solid rapture when she spoke. From the day she started at work, I had felt it. From the very beginning I had known it, how I felt, but I didn't want to seem weird, you know? I realise it's unusual to have this strength of feeling from the outset, and I knew most people wouldn't get it. It was wonderful but terrifying. I couldn't risk the exposure, looking a fool, or mad, and I couldn't risk ruining it and never having a chance.

So, I'd played the long game. I'd been the friend. I'd moved slowly, carefully, planning my moves.

This wasn't meant to happen. This wasn't in the plan.

'Hey?' She prompted, looking a little irked now, cross even.

'Sorry, yeah. Of course. It's exciting. I was just hesitating because of what you were saying on Friday. But I guess it was the Pinot talking,' I chuckled.

'Friday?' She asked, a little pinch between her brows.

'You know, about him being a bit, a bit much sometimes.'

'I said that? Did I? I don't think I did,' she was looking at the floor, then around the room. Looking for an answer. A memory.

'Well, yeah. You said he was, I think the word was 'overbearing'. You were talking about him being a bit sort of controlling. Remember? We were sat at the bar, after the others had gone. Remember? Anyway, it doesn't matter, it was really late and we'd both had a skin-full by then.' I chuckled.

I wondered if I'd gone too far.

A blanket had fallen over us. I wanted to shift the awkwardness on. I wanted to shake it away. I didn't want to be talking any more. I wanted to leave, to collect my thoughts.

'Oh,' she said. 'I really don't recall that.'

Her beautiful, green eyes were squinting now.

'But I do think it's a good idea,' she said, quietly, 'moving in together, it's the next logical step, really. And it makes financial sense too.'

'How romantic!' I laughed, standing, and I gently pressed her right shoulder as I walked past her. I squeezed her right shoulder as I always did, as I loved to do, so that the impression of her bones and skin would stay on me for the rest of the day. I would feel it, could almost see it. Like an imprint in the snow.

I was still raw when she had started at work. I was raw and full of fury. It had only been six months since that business with Jayne and not a day went by when I didn't think if her, think of all that happened, think of all that had happened to me. It was a heavy weight, and the encumbrance of it, the crush of it, meant I wasn't really myself back then. I was withdrawn, preoccupied. I guess depressed, really. I hadn't quite seen what Jayne had done to me at the time. I suppose that's a skill some people have.

Then, when she arrived, I was lifted again. It was that simple.

So now, I couldn't bear knowing that it was never going to happen. But worse, to be with him.

I saw her sometimes when she arrived in the morning, harassed, and I knew she was upset. Some days her make-up was not quite perfect, she hadn't done her eyeliner in that way she did - or her hair was down and not pinned up, just brushed through. I knew it, on those days. You could see it written large across her face. She was drawn, tired. She would talk to me, and then I would know they'd argued. She'd allude to it, but never spell it out. She was too loyal. And I would just let her talk, I didn't ask, I listened. And I could hear it, I could hear it in her voice and I could hear it in the missing words. It was painful.

So even if it couldn't be me, it shouldn't be him.

I needed to help her. I needed to help her get out of that mess before it went any further.

Later that day, she walked past my desk. On it, I had a Toblerone. Her favourite.

'Oo. Can I...?' She asked, stretching her pale, long arm across my desk, across my own, to reach it. She was bending low across me. I could feel soft warmth.

'So, when's the big day?' I asked, trying hard to sound chirpy.

She snorted, 'You make it sound like a wedding!'

'Well, that'll be next!' I laughed, lightly touching her arm before she took it back. Near her wrist was a small brown bruise.

'It really won't be,' she said, firmly. But with a hint of a smile.

The next day, he came in. Mid-morning, he turned up, two coffees in hand. She'd been quiet until then, a little withdrawn. Her outfit was plain black; she usually wore print, at least one printed thing. I had wondered if something had happened, but too many people were around. I didn't want to impose or ask her when the others were there. It didn't seem fair.

He came in and then she was laughing. His whole presence was loud – he had a bright green polo shirt on, too much aftershave, too much noise. He was teasing her. The coffee scent was around them and they were inside a bubble together; a bead, a blister. Everyone else was looking in. They wanted to be inside, to be in there. You could sense people yearning for it.

But I felt sad for her, at the illusion of it, and the gap between the appearance and the reality.

I centred myself, and slowly stood up, walked over.

'Can you believe some bastard did her car, eh? Has she told you?'

I flinched.

'No? What's happened?' I looked at her, tried to catch her eye. She was quiet again. I knew she was unhappy.

'Someone's keyed her car. Scratched it up. The driver's side. Not just once though, tiger stripes there are. Deliberate.'

I looked at her again, willing her to meet my gaze. I reached one hand up, was going to touch her, thought better of it. My hand stayed in the air a moment, lost, hovering.

'Oh my God. Are you OK?' I asked. 'Where did it happen; where were you parked?' I asked.

'She was at mine. Staying over, weren't you?' He rubbed her upper back, a little too hard. I felt the touch as my own.

And there it was, the hint of smugness. She was at his. Would it become theirs? Or would it always be his, I wondered. Would she be a guest in her own home? And I didn't like his voice; the moves.

'That's terrible.' I stated. I dropped my arm. 'I hope you've reported it to the Police.

'Mind you, they are next to useless with things like that. I had a camera stolen from the back of my car once. It was worth 500 quid, but they did bugger all.

'God, I wonder who did it?' I said, staring at Tom. He met my eyes; he gave a confident smile.

You sod.

Across the office, Steph came in, so I used it as an excuse to move off – I went to talk to her. I couldn't stay there with them, in that space, and with that noise and smell and hurt.

His place. His place was in Smithstown. Supposedly up and coming, but hadn't made it all the way up yet, in my opinion. I would tell her that later, try to drop it in, to get her to see. That wasn't a great place to live. She would be better off staying where she was. Not only would she be with him, she'd be in a rough neighbourhood. The whole thing was unbearable.

The following Monday, she came in wearing a new dress and with long earrings on, much longer than she would usually wear. They were almost skimming her shoulders. With her hair up but soft little curls falling around her face, she looked whimsical, bohemian. It suited her. And she was upbeat.

'Fancy grabbing some lunch today?' I asked. 'My treat!'

'Why not?' she replied, gently smiling, 'One o'clock?'

Throughout the morning, I was restless, worried. Of course, she looked happier today but the things she'd mentioned in the last week alone had done nothing to appease my concerns. She talked about not getting much sleep when some party-goers had disturbed her, being noisy in the street outside his house; she'd complained he'd been late to collect her from work last Thursday. But worst, she'd mentioned him being grumpy after his team lost at football – it was a guarded, euphemistic conversation. When I'd gently pressed her on it, she'd backed down, shut down. I was pretty sure I knew what being 'grumpy' entailed.

We sat across from each other at lunch; bowls of soup steaming on the table.

'So, did you get up to anything exciting at the weekend?' I asked, eyebrow raised. It was an opening for her, a cue. I was a good listener. I always let her dominate, always. It was a conscious thing. I wanted her to see what she could have from someone else, someone who didn't take over the way he did.

'Oh, we went out on Friday, with some people from Tom's work. Jo and Chris. It was quite a late one really. I'm getting too old.'

She smiled, and I gave a little grimace and shake of the head, trying to indicate no she was not, but also, yes, me too.

'I think you've told me about them before. The ones who you find annoying?'

She looked surprised.

'Yes, I suppose they can be. Anyway, Tom got leathered, really drunk. He was so bad he still felt rough by Saturday evening. We were meant to be going to the cinema and we had to put it off.' I thought I could hear something in her voice. Something I didn't like.

'That doesn't sound good.' I said.

'Oh no, it was fine. I didn't care, really.'

But she was looking in her soup, lifting spoonfuls of it up and dropping it back into the bowl, absentmindedly. She sounded odd, far away; hidden inside her words there was a truth. And inside that truth there was pain.

'We should go out.' I found myself saying, suddenly. 'Me and you.'

'You make it sound unusual,' she said, 'but we go out all the time!'

'No, not with that lot. Just me and you. To dinner or something. This Friday. Let's do it.'

She paused, and the soup dripped slowly back into her bowl as she tipped the spoon.

'Yes, I'd like that,' she said.

By Friday, I was a tightly coiled spring. I'd been to get a new outfit, had a haircut. I'd booked a lovely Italian; spent an age reflecting on it. I wanted somewhere cosy and special but not too flash. I thought I'd found it.

She came in to work with her hair down, but straightened, with the front clipped back. She looked lovely. I managed to keep myself from talking to her all day. I restrained myself. Until the end of the day, when everyone was packing up. I strolled over, asked her if she had 'a home to go to'. She swivelled her chair around and gave me a soft smile.

'Shall I pick you up tonight then, or are you getting the bus?'

She looked shocked.

'Tonight? What's tonight?'

Or was it something else. Did she look defensive? Nervous?

'Dinner. You and me. Tonight. Remember?' I was chuckling but not laughing, grinning but not smiling.

Was it cagey?

'Oh, did we say tonight? I had completely forgotten!' she said. 'I'm so sorry, I can't.'

Or was it scared.

And she actually started to turn her chair back towards her desk, to lift her arm out for her mouse. A deliberate movement. On the back of her neck I saw a tiny scratch. In her posture I felt tension. In her words I heard fear. She was trying to tell me something without saying it. She was telling me.

'Wait, you're saying you *can't*.' I said firmly.

'No, sorry.' She muttered, not making eye contact. She was pretending to work, pretending to already be back at work. I knew what it was. She was trapped.

The ground was falling away from me so I moved quickly, I walked away, walked as the ground fell down around me, walked across a pathway, stepping stones, a causeway; wobbling, at risk of falling. Falling. I kept going. I walked away from her, and kept going, straight out of the building, straight towards the car park.

I took the keys from my pocket and scratched.

The Best Things

He looked at her and blinked slowly, but did not reply.

'…Excuse me, could I have a small pot of Earl Grey tea?' she repeated.

Behind the counter, the muscular young man continued to stare. The slightest hint of a smirk played around his lips - but he did not move. For a moment they both stood still, facing each other, and then slowly and deliberately he raised one arm high, to bring a large, flat hand, palm up, close to her face. A dead fish.

'£2.50,' he said.

The sounds popped out like pebbledash.

She jumped slightly and started her little ritual of searching through her handbag for the correct change. £2.50 was a little more than she had expected. There was a time when you could buy a whole cream tea for £2.50. £2.50! But then… time passes, the world moves on, things change.

She counted out her coins awkwardly, dropping receipts and pennies as she went, embarrassed now to see the queue slowly forming behind her. A woman nearby sniffed, pointedly. A child stared. The young man behind the counter remained stock still - arm out, face impassive. She brought each coin close to her face to check the worth and then, one by one, dropped them into his palm.

When she had finished he simply jerked his head towards the empty tables nearby and placed the coins in the till. He did not look at her again.

She bent down to pick up the pile of bags at her feet and carried them over to the nearest table. She could hear her feet dragging as she went, and made a conscious effort to lift them from the floor and walk more gracefully. A fleeting image of Peter darted through her head.

Don't shuffle, Connie.

Once settled in her chair she pushed her bags under the table and sat with her hands in her lap, waiting for the tea. The bags rustled and settled onto the floor around and across her feet, like a litter of puppies. Her tartan purse sat neatly in front of her. She was hoping for a china cup; for £2.50 she should get a china cup. She tried not to dwell on the fact she only had 20 pence left in her purse - she didn't want anything to mar her enjoyment of the tea, when it finally came. She had earned it, walking the high street this morning. So many people. So much noise.

In front of her hung a huge, rectangular mirror with a heavy, silver frame. As her eyes settled into focus she took in the image of herself, reflected back. She looked old, tired, a little scruffy. (Sort yourself out, Connie.) On her left cheek the wound from last week's incident was still raw – a large bruise mingled with a gash, dark purply red, crushed raspberries. No wonder the young man behind the counter had been so peculiar towards her. She had actually forgotten it was there.

The tea was here – it came with a mug. Not even a cup and saucer. A small, crisp biscuit sat cellophane-wrapped on the tray; she took it and slipped it into her purse.

Suddenly, a little boy was at her side, standing close and beaming. His almond-shaped eyes danced as he said, 'I've got a penny,' and he unfolded one, podgy hand to reveal a pound coin.

'My, that's lovely. You lucky boy!' she declared, 'You must have been a very good boy to get that.'

He grinned but did not answer, continuing to stare down into his hand.

'I've got one, too,' she said.

She unclipped the clasp of her purse and searched among her receipts for her last remaining coin. Small treasures spilled onto the table; the biscuit; a mint wrapped in crinkled paper; a safety pin; a photo; a button. Her best things.

'Who's that?' the boy said, pointing at her photo with his one free hand.

'That's my daughter,' she said, 'my daughter when she was your age. How old are you sweetheart? Six?'

He didn't answer but said, 'Who's the other one? Who's the man?'

He peered closer, fascinated by the small black and white image.

'He's gone,' she said. She didn't want to look at the picture.

'Gone where?'

'Just gone.'

'Is your daughter gone, too?' he asked, standing so close she could feel his sweet breath on her face.

She leaned into him: his jammy smell. Then she put the photo away.

'What are you going to do with your money?' she asked.

'You look sad,' he stated. 'Do you want my penny?'

'Bless you,' she said, touched.

Then his mother appeared and grabbed him by the arm. She did not make eye contact with Connie but tugged him away through the tables, muttering quickly and softly to him. Connie could not hear what was said. Something about strangers, no doubt. The boy looked back at her the whole time, not listening, but grinning, and continued to hold his right hand out with a fist clenched around his pound coin, waving it, waving the whole arm.

'What happened to your face?' he called back to her.

Outside, the sun was finally beginning to shine. Shards of light broke through the blinds across the tablecloths and she was tempted up and out again, even though her legs ached in their stockings and she felt too warm in her woollen coat. She only had 20 pence left. Enough for a phone call perhaps, nothing more.

She gathered her bags together and weaved slowly through the tables to the exit. The young man behind the counter stood and watched, arms folded, as she struggled to open the door, body and hands laden. She had to place some things at her feet and then various random items began to roll from her favourite shopping bag, the one with a pale, blue checked pattern and dotted with pink roses, spilling out across the floor in a slowly, erupting mess.

Look what you've done Connie, you stupid woman.

'Thank you,' she said quietly to the elderly gentleman who suddenly appeared at her side to hold the door as she gathered her things, gathered herself, back together. 'Thank you very much,' she could not meet his eyes. She was ashamed.

'Manners cost nothing,' he said, loudly, to the room.

In the street outside the café, two or three people stood huddled near a violinist who was playing, beautifully. Bach, if she was not mistaken. He swayed as he played, eyes shut, absorbed. An image of her daughter came to her, learning to play the viola, aged nine. Perhaps she should call her. Maybe it was not too late.

(Do you have to let her make that infernal racket, Connie?)

Transfixed by the music she forgot the weight of her bags and the heaviness of her legs, the warmth of the sun and the heat of her coat. It was, simply, beautiful. As he finished the piece the passers-by drifted away, and she searched for her purse, and her 20 pence piece. The violinist tucked his bow in the crook of his arm and with his left hand, wrapped long, white fingers around her own as she fumbled with the clasp. He held his hand over hands gently, enveloping hers, and the purse within it. He shook his head gently at her, and smiled softly.

'No money, please,' he said, in an Eastern European accent.

She nodded her head.

A gang of men in tracksuits and caps came by, some holding cans of lager or bottles of beer, all shouting, red faced, raucous. One stopped when he saw her.

'Whaay! What did the other guy look like, eh? The other guy, what'd 'e look like? Twat him with one of your shopping bags, did you?' he rocked on his feet in front of her. He had one tooth missing at the front, and a spot of dribble on his chin. She noticed a small stain in the crotch of his trousers, a miniature map of China.

'I'm sorry, I beg your pardon?' she asked.

Unexpectedly, this seemed to anger him.

''I beg your pardon!' 'I beg your pardon!' Who the hell you think you are, like some bloody… like some…f'sake…' he paused, searching for the words he wanted. 'YOU DISGUST ME.'

With each word he nodded slightly, emphatically, and swayed closer towards her.

'Look. At. You,' he said.

There was a pause, and a stillness, like the tide pulling back on the beach. She thought back to last week, to the incident. She wondered how she managed to get into these situations, still. She should know by now. She should know how not to rile them.

(Why do you make me so angry with you, Connie? Why do you do it?)

And then the still was shattered as the violinist stepped forward slightly, forward and to the side, half blocking his path in subtle act of protection.

He said, simply, 'She is old woman.'

The man snorted and walked away, towards his friends who were laughing and leering nearby. One slapped him on his shoulders as he approached.

'Thank you,' she said and took out her purse to find the 20 pence piece. This time he did not stop her.

On her way home, she could feel the warmth of the afternoon sun dissipating and began wondering if it would be a cold night. She kept her head down, avoiding all eyes, trying to avoid any more difficulties. It had been a long day. The bags pulled down on her arms, the plastic handles cutting into her hands. She thought of the little boy in the café, the man who held the door for her, the music, the violinist, the thug, the incident last week, the purple flag on her cheek. She thought of Peter. She thought of her daughter.

As she approached the door she paused next to a young woman who was out in the street buried in a sleeping bag, curled tight, but with eyes open, fearful and watching straight ahead. A small, white dog was curled in the curve of her abdomen. Connie put down her bags again.

'Excuse me, Grace,' said Connie, 'Grace, I got you this.'

She pulled out the biscuit from her purse, now snapped but still encased in its wrapper. Grace did not move. Connie bent down and placed it gently on the folds of her sleeping bag, then picked up her bags again and wandered the last few paces towards her doorway.

Her cardboard was still there; her cardboard and newspaper. She was lucky. She placed her bags in a small heap together, bent herself down and onto the step. Slowly, she began to construct her cardboard defences around her; her makeshift walls; her home. She lay the newspaper down (every bed needs sheets, she said to herself) retaining some for extra warmth later. She pulled out her blanket from the bottom of her favourite shopping bag - the one with a pale, blue checked pattern and dotted with pink roses. She lay down on the paper and placed the bag under her head as a pillow. She twisted the clasp of her purse, slipping out the photograph, covering Peter's image with one thumb and nuzzling her daughter's image into her cheek.

Perhaps she would call her tomorrow. Perhaps.
It would only cost 20 pence.

Social Animal

The forum post said: *Whot do u do when baby wont stop crying my baby crys all night all the time please HELP.* And then, next to it, a little cartoon image of a weeping face. From BusieB.

He smiled. He could feel words of advice spring forth effortlessly, and he itched to write. His fingertips twitched. This one was easy. He knew exactly how to help.

He made himself stop and savour the moment. He looked down at the screen, as the notification changed, informing him the post had been made 'just now' to, shortly, 'one min', 'three mins', and then 'five mins'. He forced himself to watch and wait for a full ten minutes: staring at the screen, scrolling down as the post began to get buried among the others – but he was not interested in those. He had his prize in mind: kept it in view, all the time, waiting.

There was no response to her query; poor lamb.

His patience was like a little boy, waiting for cake. A birthday; a candle; a present.

It was time. The satisfaction of replying gave a flood of euphoria; a temporary release. He hit send; sat back.

Now for a cup of tea.

Work today, before he had come home, had been tedious as usual. Unsatisfying. The drudgery of entering numbers into a database was only mildly lifted by the challenge of a short coding exercise in the afternoon. He had to weigh up the vague excitement of achieving something for once, with the knowledge that he should string it out and work slowly, to take a bit longer, to avoid going back to inputting. So, while it might sound odd, this habit, this hobby, it filled a little gap. And it would be better - of course it would be better - if the day job gave him this boost, but at the moment he could see no opportunity for this to happen. Instead, he focussed his energies where he knew he would get results.

The fastest way from A to B is not always in a straight line.

Ha! He'd have to remember that one for later.

Mug in one hand, plate of biscuits in the other, he came back to the dining table and examined his phone. His post had received fifteen reactions and three comments already. Nice. Nothing from the original poster though.

Next.

He moved onto another page. Played a round a little. A meme here and there, but nothing too sensational. Then he posted a few sentences on a forum about wellbeing – essentially a support group by another name. It had 40K+ members. Forty thousand people, so low or lonely that they would turn to strangers for advice. It was astounding.

Suziey Tee was a regular poster on the site. *I feel so sad now I don't know what to do, some1 please give me advise?*

He stopped and looked at the screen. Did people really think the answer was here? In this little, grey room? He stopped to contemplate an answer. He wanted to make this one full, detailed, a considered response. A site like this: it deserved it.

He finished his cup of tea and reflected. To give himself more time, he went into the kitchen and refilled the kettle. Suziey deserved a crafted reply. He rolled some words around in his mouth to consider before typing, as he moved around the room, taking his noodle cup from the cupboard as the kettle boiled, getting himself his favourite fork from the sink.

'Demoralised,' he said.

'Dejected,' he considered.

'Disconsolate!' he announced, cheerily. Excellent.

He poured hot water into the pot and opened a sachet of Soy Sauce, squirted it across the top. Then back to his phone. He had to log back in again.

The noodles were soft and swollen, thin and tangled as bladder wrack as he sat back down at the table.

Suziey, there are thousands of people on this site just like you… he began. As he continued to type he took his time, edited as he went, waited a little while before he hit send. He was pleased with his reply, which was a full paragraph of text sitting solidly and confidently among the platitudes.

He turned, then, to the 'Slow Cooker Forum' for a bit of light relief, scrolling through reams and reams of recipes, posts and advice. For a brief moment he considered tipping his noodles into a bowl and posting it, seeing if anyone realised - but he knew this was ridiculously childish. Instead, he gave a few random reactions to people on the page and scanned the forum for something worthy of comment.

His phone bleeped with a text and broke his concentration. Just his brother: he could wait. Irritated that this had altered the mood, he stood and took his empty noodle cup and his fork into the kitchen. He dropped the waste in the bin and grabbed a beer from the fridge. Another bleep from his phone. Bloody messages. He knew what it would be: it was mum's birthday in four days, one of the few times a year when they all got together. Dave would be trying to firm up the plans that he had so far managed to leave as deliciously vague. He was not in the mood right now; he was still thinking about Suziey, wondering if he should go back to the page and see what was happening. Whether he should go back to add some more.

He was busy.

'Devastated,' he said aloud.

'Traumatised?' he wondered. No – perhaps too dramatic. Even for the internet.

He snorted.

He took his beer back into the other room, but forced himself not to pick up his phone. He went over to the sofa and sat in his spot. Not that anyone else had a spot in this room: he couldn't even remember the last time someone else was in here. Though he couldn't say that he particularly minded. He didn't feel lonely exactly, though sometimes a little bored.

He picked up his music magazine from where it fallen onto the floor a couple of days ago. He flicked through, stopping to read the one-star reviews and the letters' page. It was amusingly scathing about anything and everyone. He downed the final dregs of his beer. He was inspired.

He wandered back to the kitchen, dropped his empty beer bottle next to the bin and grabbed another one from the fridge. On the way back to the sofa he picked up his phone, logging back in to the page on his way.

'Local Musicians and Groups' was a small-ish group with only 46 members, but it sometimes had some interesting posts. He hadn't been on it for a while. He took a look now. There didn't seem to have been much action at all recently, not much since the huge row that had taken place on there, around two weeks earlier.

He looked back through, to a thread of comments with 52 posts attached. Exclamation marks like dead ants littered the screen. Some comments seemed to have been removed as the argument no longer made sense. It was simply two people angrily agreeing with each other while a third impotent and silent enemy was conspicuous by his absence. He fiddled around on the page – scrolled through images and added a word here or there. Then he ran his fingers up the page until he found his place back to the top.

Now, at the top of the page he added a new post – by his account, WonderStevie72.

Went 2 see the Battle of The Bands on weekend. Great big pile of turds, it said.

He paused. Waited for some sort of reaction. Sure enough, a little angry face appeared on the post, instantly.

Success.

He grinned, logged out, logged back in again; quickly found the page. Refocussed his mind. Took a deep breath and considered his voice.

WonderStevie72, he typed this time, *have some respect, mate? Some of those guys were practicly kids. Shame on you, mate. I for one enjoyed it.*

Almost simultaneously, another post appeared below his, a new voice, who he hadn't interacted with before: *Spoken like a true armchair air guitarist Stevie. I'll bet your last LP went platinum, right? LOL.*

He chuckled. Savoured the moment and took a swig of his beer. He had secured one. He logged back out. Paused; smiled; waited; swam inside the feeling for a little while.

'Impotent,' he declared.

'Incompetent?' he wondered.

'Inept!' he practically shouted, did a little fist pump in the air.

Then back in again: a new log in. Now he would use his favourite. Not WonderStevie this time. He needed the big guns. He carefully reflected and took a moment to recall the usual spelling, the voice.

Some people are just downright nasty, Ive come across some nasty bstrds on the internet today. Just ignor him. X x x. BusieB.

Let Me Tell You a Story

They think I have nothing to say.

Granny says that it's just a phase, and the more of a big deal everyone makes about it, the longer it will go on. Dad says I must be an idiot, because if I had two brain cells to rub together I'd have grown out of this nonsense by now. Mum doesn't mention it much. But she does cry sometimes.

I say they are all right, but at the same time all wrong – and that's confusing. But I say it in my head; a whisper in my head that talks into my own ear and nowhere else. Because it feels better that way.

Let me tell you a story.

A year or two ago, the sleeve started to come off on my favourite raincoat. Mum bought me a new one, but I threw it on the floor, and screamed. I screamed so hard and so long that my mouth tasted of blood and salt and I slipped into that mood, that feeling, where everything was closing in and black and red and I didn't really know where I was anymore. When I found out where I was again, I realised I was lying on the tiles in the kitchen, curled into a ball like a cat. I was cold. I was on my own, but I had a blanket on.

Later, In the middle of the night, I came down to get some water because my throat was filled with grit and sand. I stood on the stairs, halfway down the stairs, when I realised mum was still awake. She might have been cross with me, still, but more than that I was terrified in case dad was there. I wasn't sure what he knew. I hesitated and watched her from afar, stood still and watched as she sat on the couch with her head bent over. Crying: she was crying, quietly.

And she was sewing the sleeve back together on my old coat.

The next day, it wasn't even raining but I put that coat on all day. The torn sleeve was a little bit wonky because the buttons were in the wrong place. I used to hold them and the cuffs with the tips of my fingers but now I couldn't and so they felt strange, almost right but not quite right. And the sleeve was shorter too, shorter than the other one, than it should have been. But I didn't care enough about it for it to make me scream, and I didn't want to see mum cross or sad again. And I was scared of what dad would say. I wore it inside and outside the house. I even wore it at the dinner table. Dad didn't speak to me, said nothing at all about it and I was relieved.

You see, I feel like I am that coat sometimes. Almost right, but not quite right. Almost myself, yet not. Stitched up and sewn back together, a little bit wrong. And everyone else can see it. They can see the stitches, where I am broken.

When I was really little, I did talk sometimes. Mum reminds everyone of this quite often. Sometimes she says it to shut people up: people who think I am stupid, like dad. Other times she says it almost to herself, sort of confused. And occasionally, she says it in desperation: to Doctors, and teachers, and other people who are supposed to help us.

I used to say 'hi', 'bye-bye', 'cup' and a few different foods, apparently. I used to say 'no'.

I used to say 'mum'.

When I started school, I found it even harder. The words were there but I felt like I was swimming and they were in the water all around me, muddled up and floating away. And if someone wanted me to speak, if they asked me a question, I could feel the words dissolving into a sea of letters. And I could feel my skin throbbing and my jaw hurting and I usually said nothing. A few times I tried, and I said the wrong word, or it sounded weird and the other children giggled - and that just made it worse.

Mum was shocked when they told her. Dad said they were 'talking crap'. You see, I was still talking a bit at home at that time, and they simply didn't believe them.

In the end, the school asked mum to come in and see. She sat at the teacher's chair and watched, and I pretended I didn't know and I pretended she wasn't there - but I knew she was. I sat on my own and looked at the table and drew circles on the piece of paper they had given me to draw a picture of my family. I drew small circles, smaller and smaller, until they were tiny and perfect, like bubbles. Like foam. A few times, the teacher tried to speak to me, to persuade me to use a different colour or draw my mum or my cat, or my Granny. But I carried on staring at the paper, drawing circles. In the end, she left me alone and walked away.

Then we were supposed to tell the person next to us about our picture. I looked at the boy while he explained his to me. I thought his family sounded odd and I wondered where his mum was in the picture, but I just gave a little smile and stared at the page. Then it was my turn, and I kicked my legs out and under again lots of times, and looked at the floor. The blood was in my ears and the letters were in the air and I kept my mouth closed.

Then it was the end of the day and mum was talking to the teacher. She was angry, but I couldn't tell who with. The teacher was saying words like 'assessments' and 'specialists' and 'funding' and mum was just shaking her head at everything and then she grabbed me by the wrist and marched me out of the school.

I remember a woman came in a few times in the weeks and months that followed that, and she took me into Mrs Simon's office – which was really a cupboard – and started trying to make me say and do things while she made lots of notes on forms and bits of paper. She was trying to force my brain and mouth into shapes and things they did not want to do. But I am not clay.

Then after that, soon after that, one day mum came back in again and I was glad at first, because they let us play a game together in the corner of the classroom. This was good as they usually just tried to make me write three letter words on a table on my own, where I just scribbled hard on the page, because I didn't see the point. So, when mum came in and we had a game I was delighted; I even whispered 'me' a couple of times when it was my turn, and mum beamed and looked so happy, and I was, too.

Then she nodded at the teacher and they pushed over another girl, Kimmie, to play and she sat on the empty chair between us and tried to join in, so I knocked my counters on the floor very slowly, one by one, and then stared at the carpet between my swinging legs, where the counters had settled, like the planets on a map of the sky.

After this, I didn't speak at school at all.

The very last day I had there, was a day that makes me feel peculiar to think about. I'm not sure I can tell that story very well. My tummy goes weird. They were leaving me alone by then and I was sat in the book corner, looking through a little pile of books Mrs Thompson had given me. They were very easy books with only one or two words on a page and thick cardboard pages, for a baby, I thought. They always gave me books like these. I was trying to amuse myself, so I was staring at the colours in the pictures, staring hard until my eyes went funny, trying to get the colour in my head or my head in the colour when I spotted that someone had put an envelope with my name on, at my feet. I hadn't even noticed them do it. I get locked inside my thoughts sometimes. I took it and looked at it.

My head felt suspicious, wondering what the trick was, but I told it to shut up. My head can be very tiring. Sometimes it's nice just to get on with things and stop thinking.

Inside was a little voucher. It said 'sweets' and a there was a picture of a pile of sweets.

Miss Leeman, the helper teacher, came over. She bent over towards me, smiling.

'All you have to do is go over to Mrs Simon and ask her for the sweets, and they're yours. We got strawberry shoelaces. Your mum says they are your favourite,' she said.

Her voice was kind. But her words made me feel sick.

I didn't have sweets very often. Dad was strict, said I needed rules to 'sort me out'. I looked over to Mrs Simon's desk. She was sat there, staring at me, and then slowly she opened her top drawer and took out a bag of strawberry laces. She held them up in one hand and continued to stare. She smiled, but she didn't look happy.

'I dare you,' her face seemed to be saying to me.

It reminded me of dad, somehow.

Suddenly, I threw the book that was in my hand hard, across the carpet, and it hit Billy on the arm; the corner bashed him just above the wrist and there was a pause – the whole room took in a breath - before he wailed. Mrs Simon and Miss Leeman ran over to him.

And that was the last time I went to school.

I hadn't realised that was all I had to do to make it stop. I didn't know that there was something better I could have, something else to come, and I had gone on with school for so long that by the time I had the good news - that I was staying at home with mum - I was already messed up and cracked and broken. I was a bit worried it was too late.

Dad didn't really look at me in the eye after that. He said I needed a special school. One for 'slow children', he said. He didn't want me at home. He said it wasn't normal. He said I wasn't normal.

One time, when I was younger, we went for a fancy lunch and I remember having a big bowl of tomato soup - huge, hot. I didn't want it, but I was hungry, and I didn't want dad to shout at me, so I ate it. I ate it all. And then afterwards, after they took my bowl away, they came back with a plate of sausages and mash. And I didn't know, I didn't realise the soup was just the beginning and that I had sucked it up and had so much of it that I was too full for the next course, even though it should have been the best part.

That's how I felt about school. And home. You see?

So, then I stayed home, and I painted. I painted circles and sometimes lines. Mum bought me bright colours and I mixed them with water to make the page as wet as I could. Sometimes I wrote, too, but I did it in my notebook in my bedroom and I put it in a box at the bottom of my wardrobe, and I didn't let anyone see because I didn't want them to send me back to school to make me write my letters.

I didn't say any words, except in my head to my own ear, and mum didn't try to make me.

Dad, when he was home, acted like I was not there.

Granny came around to see mum and me at least once a week. She gave me nice, tight hugs when she talked to me, and I thought she knew what my answers were even though she couldn't hear them. We understood each other. And sometimes, I heard snippets of what they were saying about me. Because when you don't speak, people forget you are there. They forget you can hear. They talked about me and whether I was 'any better'.

'But look at her,' Granny said one Saturday, 'look at her with that book,'

I was reading The Hobbit. I had my face close to the page to make the words go into my head more securely and I was trying to make sure I understood everything because there were a few tricky ones. I tried not to stop reading just because they were staring at me as I liked the story.

'She's not really reading. You can't read if you can't speak,' dad said.

He said the words like they were like stones, or tiny bullets. They shot out across the room at speed.

Granny looked at him and frowned. Then he looked across at me and grimaced, pulled his top lip back slightly. She watched, and shook her head.

'What a stupid thing to say,' she said, quietly, 'sometimes I think it's you who's the idiot,'

I giggled, and everyone looked at me, shocked, and for a second, I saw pure joy flick across mum's face. I snapped my head back to my book, and snapped my mouth back shut. I heard dad storm out the room, the door reverberating after he barged through it.

Granny stayed for a long time that day, and she and mum had hushed conversations in the kitchen while they tidied up, and then made shepherd's pie together in synchronised movements. There was a constant stream of whispering like a flow of water, a trickling tap of ideas, concerns, thoughts. After a while I tuned it out and managed to focus on my reading.

Dad was nowhere to be seen, and nobody said anything about that.

She even stayed until bedtime, which was unusual, but nice. She ran my bath and helped me in it and stayed with me and chattered while I played with my little boat and smashed the bubbles between my hands. The water was warm and deep and sleepy. Then she wrapped me in an enormous towel and hugged me while I was still inside it, to dry me. She leant her forehead against mine and kissed my nose. It was nice.

We walked back along the corridor together to my room and found mum sitting on my bed. The wardrobe door was open and on the floor was a pile of clothes, dropped in a heap, shocked, still on their hangers. My box was open, and in her hand was my note book.

Mum must have heard us enter, but it took her a long time to look up from the page. She stared at me with an expression on her face that I had never seen before.

'Did you write this? Is this really your story?' she said.

Granny put her hands on my shoulders and held me tight. Tight.

I smiled, I nodded, I looked at her - and in a dozen ways I said *yes*, *yes*, without ever saying a word.

White Light

When he was twenty-nine, he had walked into the nursery to find Peter, cold. His skin was pale with a blue tinge, like skimmed milk. The vision of his beautiful, perfect face, now touched by the grotesque, was seared in his mind. Even now, so very many years later, he had to steel himself before each time he turned the handle on a door.

Life is a terrorist. And she is cruel.

These memories always came back whenever he visited a hospital. The smell of the place, the harsh lighting, the reverberation on the hard surfaces. He recalled walking swiftly down many corridors alongside Jean, her raw fear palpable, his machismo brutal and unnecessary, yet somehow expected at the time.

And rehearsal is the opposite of reaction: he was acting a part he had played many times before, while she was experiencing a feeling she had never dreamt she would feel. That she could not even have imagined to exist.

Today, there was no fear. At this time of life, it was less and less surprising to be sat in a hospital corridor, as he had been here many times before. When Jean was first diagnosed, he remembered the feeling vividly: like his skin was ripped apart, the terror peppered his body, burrowed deep into his pores - and he walked around like this, ruptured and damaged, for weeks, for several months. But your body and mind cannot sustain this. And like things often do, this became normal, their new normal.

He lost count of how many appointments they had, how many conflicting and confusing messages they received, shrinking and expanding timelines and predictions - until he wondered which he dreaded more: the end, or the uncertainty. Eventually, he had decided, consciously, to be brave. To stand up against his fear and stare it down. And he did.

His pocket buzzed. He knew it would be a message from Suzie. He knew, because she was the only one who ever messaged him. The one who had bought him the phone.

He took the mobile from his pocket and looked at the small, grey screen. Clumsily, he pressed the tiny, raised keys. He had taken the phone, accepted the offering grudgingly and with mild annoyance at the time, but now he was used to it and he refused to change it.

'An upgrade,' she had said.

'But why?' he had asked.

She had simply smiled and very softly shook her head.

Let me know how it goes please x x

Suzie. Four years younger than Peter. Than Peter would have been. He was not here, but she was still a younger sister, because he had been. He had been here. They refused to forget Peter, as everyone seemed to want them to. They would never do that.

His death had opened up an imperceptible fissure between him and Jean. It was tiny, almost indiscernible, but they both knew it was there. You cannot truly trust another person when you lose your trust in life itself.

That fissure, at times, had been a canyon. In his youth, he had been a very slim man, and an athlete. He had worked with his body and his body had responded with sinewy arms and a slender frame. He played soccer, too. He was light on his feet, could bound upstairs, pick Jean up and lift and spin her without a second thought. And he and Jean were entangled so closely they became one being.

After Peter left them, he had no desire to play soccer, no urge to bound or lift or spin. He slept in his chair; frequently, in the evening, often on a Sunday afternoon, and sometimes even through the night. They slept apart and fractured into two.

And he ate. Starch, white food: bread, rice, potatoes. He had seconds every time, and even thirds. He had biscuits in the afternoon and cake after his tea. Jean fried him bread and eggs for breakfast, diligently obeying his requests without comment. He was filling the gap, the void, this fissure in the only way he knew.

If you drink too much, they call you an alcoholic. If you work too hard, a workaholic. There is no name for someone who is addicted to food. You know what they call you if you eat too much? Greedy.

The world can be a judgemental place, sometimes.

Then the angina came, and he ignored it. The stomach ulcer flared and yelled at him, and he imagined it transitory, a phase. His knees complained – but he did not answer their plea. Until the heart attack came. And that was a tap on the shoulder from death.

But she was unwanted. She was early.

So finally, he listened.

He was big now, but not as big, and better, fitter. He had margarine, not butter. Seconds of veg but nothing else. Tried to move, keep moving, even as he aged.

The lights above him had an almost imperceptible flicker and his awareness of them brought him back into the room. He had always hated these white lights. Harsh, neon. Jean joked that they made her look even sicker than she was when they sat, and waited, in these corridors.

He looked down at his watch and with a sudden jolt realised he had forgotten to feed Boris. He'd be climbing the walls by the time he got home. He wasn't the most affectionate cat, but he had his routines, and he knew when it was time to be fed.

Maybe he should start setting himself alarms for this. It wasn't the first time he had forgotten, of late. It was a fairly new responsibility for him and it annoyed him that he couldn't master this one silly little thing. Jean had always fed him. But when Jean got sick, he started to offer, and then she was in and out of hospital, or in and out of bed, and a new pattern emerged where it was now his job somehow. And it was this little thing that made him realise how impotent he was around the home. She did everything for him. He was angry at his own ineffectiveness (he struggled even to use the can opener for the cat-food) and angry – furious - that he had never noticed and appreciated her, until she was simply too ill to look after him anymore.

So now Suzie took him shopping for microwave meals and soup in cartons once a week, a cleaner came around every Monday to hoover, and help with the washing and ironing - and around once a month his friend Jeff extended an invite for a Sunday lunch. At first, Jean resisted these new interventions. She saw it for what it was – the beginning of the end. But eventually she was too ill to care.

A nurse came out of the room opposite him, suddenly. He looked up, startled. She gave him a little smile, her dark, tightly curled hair sprang out from the sides of her hat as a curlicue. She was shockingly young. She carried on her way, was not for him. He would have to wait longer.

He was reminded of Sally. Of the love that never was. The love that almost was.

He had met her at the bar one night when he was out with his work mates. She was with her sisters, celebrating someone's birthday, if he recalled correctly. She was giddy, giggling when he saw her; had tried to pull her hair back into an up-do of sorts, in the latest style. But her hair was ferocious, wild, and was bursting out from its confines.

She was stunning.

And – much as he would love to, now, looking back - he couldn't even blame his grief, because this before it all happened. He would love to re-write the memory and tell it as a lie, but this was before Peter left them, before he was even born. Jean was pregnant, in fact, showing and glowing. He didn't know why this spark was lit. But it was.

He saw Sally then, most Fridays, though never in between. She hadn't been a regular in the bar before, but she was now. Sally, with her sheer black stockings and her red nails. Sally. With her smile.

Looking back, Jean would have known. He was not a subtle man, and not a good liar, he knew. And his poor lies, and guilt, made him angry with her, somehow. He lashed out and swore. He withdrew and was broody. Except on a Friday morning, when he could feel his body buzz and hum in anticipation. On Friday mornings, he was a charm. Jean did not deserve this.

And then Peter was born, and he spent less time in the pub.

And then Peter died, and he spent none at all.

He wondered where Sally was now – what had become of her. He had not seen her in years.

A young man, a boy, was pushed past him in a wheelchair by a porter then, and this reminded him again where he was. He had one leg out straight in front of him, his trouser leg rolled up above his knee, swollen, and he cupped both hands in his lap, lacerated and slashed with grit. He'd be OK; all fixable ailments; though if Jean were here, she'd call to him, say something comforting. She was kind like that.

The white light above him continued to buzz.

He felt that he'd been waiting an age.

He wondered what was wrong. He just wanted to be with Jean again, to see her, to tell her he loved her. He wanted some good news for once.

Next to him, was a small pile of tatty magazines. He reached down to pick one up, laughing inwardly to himself that he would never have gone near one of these just five years ago, but endless exposure to scenarios such as these had distorted his perception and boundaries. So now, yes, he did sometimes read about wives who had run off with their daughters' teenage boyfriends, or twenty-something celebrities whose marriage had broken up.

And then, just as he was about to start reading, another door opened in the corridor, facing him but to his left; a Doctor called his name, quite softly. There was really no need to even say it - he was the only one there. In his hand the Doctor was clutching a thick, pink cardboard file. And in that file, he knew, were the test results he was here to receive.

For a brief moment, he did not move, but under the harsh, white lighting examined the Doctor's face to try to anticipate the news. He thought that within the Doctor's weary smile he could sense sympathy. And that sympathy spelt hope for him. Hope that they would soon be back together: no more afternoons alone in the armchair. No more ready meals for one.

Hope that he would be joining Jean, his beautiful, wonderful Jean, once more. And Peter. That the white light would be all encompassing, call to him, absorb him.

That this was the beginning of his end.

Missing

I came into the room, to the stench of sweat and lavender. Nana and Tommy were staring at the floor, by the couch. Tommy, on his hands and knees.

'What's going on?' I asked.

'It's lost,' Nana said. Neither of them looked up. Tommy scuttled over, a beetle, to look on the ground by the arm of the chair.

'It's gone, Daddy,' he stated, still looking, urgently.

As if this would make sense.

'What has?' I asked, absently, as I walked across the room. I was as far away from them, as they were from me.

'It's GONE,' he declared, grumpily. 'We can't find it.'

'Missing,' Nana said, softly.

'Ok, then,' I muttered to myself, as I entered the kitchen.

— — —

In theory, everyone wants to think they would take care of their own family, if they needed it. I guess we want to think we are the good guys, and we want to think someone else would do the same for us. So, when you hear these stories of elderly people abused or neglected, you're shocked. And when you consider mental health problems, or senility, you believe you are patient, and tolerant and kind. You think that love transcends all. You can't believe that grown adults could be so cruel as to turn their back on their own relatives, or to abuse their own children, even. You can't believe that human beings would want to get rid of their responsibility, would be so brutal.

But I can.

I didn't, but right now, I can.

Because children can be utterly infuriating. Because people who need caring for can be horrible. Nasty, self-indulgent, erratic. And it is an endless weight. It is an endless, repetitive irritation to be around them. Imagine a woodpecker pecking at your head, and you tell it to stop, you try to train it to stop, but it won't, it won't stop. It doesn't. It goes on and on and pecks you, until you bleed – and it's all a mess, it's all a bleeding, bloody mess. Relentlessness. No end.

– – –

Quite often, when Tommy called to me, it reminded me of how I missed my Dad. He would stand too close and call too loud, 'Dad!', and I would think of him.

That was his title, his accolade, and I wasn't sure I'd earnt it yet.

It had been almost six months since he died. Not long really; not long compared to 79 years.

He was always there, in the background, in the stories Nana told (on the good days), in the painting in the kitchen, in the cowlick of Tommy's hair.

I missed him more than words.

– – –

The next day, Tommy was eating breakfast by the time I came down. Nana was sitting at the table, patiently.

'Daddy!' Tommy cried, as if he hadn't seen me in weeks.

'Hey, dude,' I answered. Ruffled his hair.

'Morning, mum,' I said.

She didn't look up, or move, but she shifted her face into a smile.

'Thank you,' she said.

'Ok, then,' I muttered, as I walked into the kitchen.

Gabbi was in the kitchen, watching an egg timer, standing there in her white nightie with a rip up the side. Standing there with hair in a broken, scruffy plait.

'What time did you get in?' she asked. She still had a faint line, like a whisper of sleep, on her left cheek.

'Didn't get the bar locked up until after twelve,' I said, 'so I guess it was probably one. Sorry, love. I didn't mean to disturb you. If we still had a spare room...'

She took a teaspoon and slapped me on the back of the hand.

'I'm just saying, life was better when we didn't have to share a bed every night,' I laughed.

'You didn't disturb me,' she said. 'You are now. Go away.' She muttered, as she turned her attention to the pan.

'It's still missing, you know,' mum stated, loudly, from the other room.

– – –

I only work three or four nights a week. Twenty-five hours, max, if I'm lucky and the punters leave late. Gabbi works forty, sometimes fifty hours. Shifts. I'm not sure she would consider this so lucky.

We're both carers, she reminds me. Both career carers. Me with my son and my mum, her with her clients.

Though she cares a lot more than I do, I think.

I mean, obviously, I do care. I love them both. Implicitly. But also, I don't *care*. You know? I'm not actually that interested. I'm immune, remote, thick skinned. I'm swathed in layers of insomnia and low self-esteem. It's a cloak, and it comforts me and disguises me.

So, I don't feel it. It just happens, and I get on with it. I do what I have to do. I guess we all do.

– – –

The following afternoon, I was hoovering when I heard a crash. I ran into the kitchen.

'What the hell?' I yelled, hands lifting to my face, grabbing by my mouth, stupid and ridiculous.

'Sorry, Daddy,' Tommy started to wail. He was on the floor, by an up-turned chair, next to a broken bowl, and a jigsaw of shattered biscuits.

'Mum, I thought you were looking after him?' I pleaded.

'Sorry. We couldn't find it,' she muttered.

And again, she was an apparition of my mum, was a trace of her.

I walked away from the scene, went back to my hoovering, left them together.

− − −

Tommy was 4 years old, but smart, you know?

Often, I thought it was that he was looking after mum, Nana, not the other way around. He would take her hand and gingerly walk in public. Like he knew, he sensed her fragility. I'd never said anything to him, but he understood.

Smart, see?

And they would play together sometimes, in their own little world.

Other times, I would find them sitting together, watching TV, him on the edge of the couch, legs dangling, and chewing the end of his thumb. She would be sitting upright, cushion wedged at her back, frowning and smiling at the television. And I would hear them laugh: hers, soft but deep, from the back of her throat, almost suppressed - his colourful and light, floating across the room to me like blossom.

I was almost jealous of them then, in those moments. And I smiled, but I always left the room.

− − −

The next weekend, I didn't even get a Friday shift. Simon's daughter was in town and he'd given her work. She'd finish Uni in a term and I had a feeling of dread that this marked the end of my 20 hrs a week. She'd be looking for work, and a 21-year-old girl was much more fun for the customers to be around than a mildly depressed, middle-aged man. Plus, of course, she was his family.

So maybe I'd lost that as well, then. The one bit of my life that didn't make me feel was bankrupt, the safe empty.

Nana was sitting in the armchair with a book on her knees, but not reading. Tommy was lying on his belly, playing with a long line of toy cars. He'd placed them bumper to bumper.

'Hey, mum,' I said.

'I can't remember where I've put it,' she replied. 'Can you?'

'Put what, mum?' I said, with gritted patience.

She didn't answer; she stared straight ahead. Tommy carried on lining up cars, an ant farm of vehicles.

'She doesn't know where it is,' he said, melodiously, almost singing.

'OK, then,' I said, and stalked out the room, quickly.

I walked into the kitchen, the kitchen I had tidied and cleaned so carefully just two hours ago, to find a surface littered with jam, crumbs, a butter dish, three plates, half eaten toast and then – bizarrely – a whole cucumber in the middle of the scene.

A carton of orange juice lay on its side, its contents spilled across the floor, and a futile attempt had been made to clear it up with a clean bath towel.

I stood still, lifted my hands to my head to steady myself. I was scared, scared of myself.

From the living room came Tommy's voice.

'Daaaad!' he yelled, 'Dad. Nana's looking in the hall cupboard for that thing again.'

– – –

When they were settled back on their couch, I cleared the floor of obstacles, got them a glass of orange each, and plumped their cushions. I found 'Dumbo' on demand and put it on for them. They sat with a bowl of chopped apple between then, captivated by stalks and elephants. I felt bereft with guilt, looking at their tired, gentle faces.

It's me, it must be me, there's something wrong with me, I thought. I must do better. I must try harder. It's hard, but try harder.

I sat for a few moments close to them, and enjoyed the still and calm.

But when I went into the downstairs toilet, a whole toilet roll greeted me, sodden and swollen, dropped down the pan.

— — —

Gabbi came home around 9.30pm, tired and smelling of deep-fried food, and despondency.

'Can I get you a cup of tea, love?' I asked.

'A red wine would do it,' she said.

She flopped onto the couch.

'Any food?'

'There's pasta left over,' I said, as I got up to walk towards the kitchen.

I just caught the look on her face as she crumpled her nose and grimaced.

'Pasta,' she muttered.

She had probably thought I wouldn't hear it.

'How about you make something yourself then, if that's not good enough for you, eh?' I snapped.

She was wounded.

'Alright,' she said, 'I was just saying. We have a lot of pasta. And I don't fancy it, right?'

She had started calmly, but by the end her voice had elevated up a notch, ended hung on a violin string.

'And I don't fancy being here every day, so I guess we all have things we don't like, don't we, *Gabbi*? But I'm doing my best, Gabbi, right? I'm doing my best!'

'What the hell's the matter with you?' she cried, 'All I said was, I don't want bloody pasta again!'

'Quiet.' I hissed. 'You'll wake them.'

One arm was slightly stretched out, after my words, pointing vaguely upstairs. Reaching out after my words, reaching out for something to clutch.

'Oh, piss off,' she stated, as she walked to the kitchen to get her wine, and Cheese and Onion crisps.

'OK, then,' I spat.

I stayed where I was. Halfway between the couch and the kitchen, not sure where to go or what to do. I could feel my heart, pounding. Hammering. Pulverising my body. And my whole body throbbed. It must have been obvious, visible. I stayed there with my arm adrift, my mind adrift, wondering how to bring myself back together again.

— — —

I woke the next day on the couch, fully clothed. My mouth was dry, my head throbbing slightly. Tommy was leaning forward into my face, confused.

'Hey, dude.' I said, gruffly.

He pointed his index finger and brought it close to my right eye. I wasn't sure why. I took my hand and wrapped my fingers around his and moved it away, irritated, trying not to be; I was trying.

Gabbi came downstairs and walked straight past me into the kitchen. I saw her as a shadow, and felt a mixture of anger and longing, fleetingly.

'Daddy,' said Tommy, 'I'm sorry, Daddy.'

'Hey, mate, don't worry. It's not your fault, mate.'

I leant forward and rested my forehead against his.

'I wet my pants,' he whispered.

— — —

Later that day, Gabbi was at work. I texted her: 'I miss u.'

Tommy was playing with his Duplo, in his usual pose, lying on his belly. He had on one shoe and one sock, and on his face was a jagged purple pen mark, that travelled from his forehead down to his jaw.

Nana, mum, was sat in her armchair. On her lap was a magazine, closed, and to her left was a cup of tea, almost cold. She sat with her hands with fingers locked together, neatly. She was just tipping into sleep. She looked thin and fragile, hollow boned.

I moved softly around Tommy, picking up his toys and dropping them into a large plastic box. He didn't notice, he was so absorbed in his building. I loved to watch him and his concentration.

Tentatively, I walked out into the lobby and opened the cupboard. The creak of the cupboard cut a slice through the still air. But they did not seem to flinch. I searched, quickly, efficiently, moving the coats apart.

Carefully, gently, I opened the front door a crack to peak outside. The taxi was waiting, the driver playing on his phone, engine on.

I took a deep breath, held the wall, steadied myself.

I took the suitcase from the cupboard.

I took a moment to turn, blew a silent kiss towards the living room, with my eyes screwed shut. Shut. A somnambulist.

'Ok, then,' I whispered to myself.

And I walked down the path towards the cab.

The Blue Hour

It was the blue hour - neither night nor morning - and the light diffused into aqua-marine particles. I turned the lamp off and the kitchen fell into shades of faded turquoise around us.

Katie and Cara sat together at the kitchen table, slowly chewing on buttered toast. I leant against the counter and watched the scene. Cara, a compact copy of her new friend.

When Katie first came along, I was not best pleased. She was an irritation. Not at all what I needed. Every time Cara mentioned her, a feeling washed over me: a billow and upsurge across my skin that would stay as a tingle, a memory, for the next hour or two. Discomfort, irritation. Grit.

Worse, when she was actually there, between us, her mere presence taunted me. I felt pressure across every inch of my body. I needed her to go away. I needed things to be as they were, and I didn't know how to make it so. Cara was reliant, enamoured, not her old self. She deferred to Katie - and I hated it.

But then, slowly, incrementally, I got used to her. I got used to her presence. I got used to being one of three.

And I started to like her.

'Who wants some more?' I asked them, gently. The indirect sunlight demanded temperate tones.

'Katie does,' Cara said, 'I don't.'

Cara looked over at Katie, side-eyed. She kicked her legs under the table, back and forth, one at a time, and a sock flapped at the end of her right foot. She knew I would want her to eat more, as she settled the crust of her slice onto her plastic plate. This was a daily battle.

'Oh, really?' I asked, raising one eyebrow. I glanced over to Katie's chair. Smiled. 'Katie's always a good girl. And she eats her crusts,' I said.

I put two more slices of toast on, leant back against the counter. I watched Cara lift a tumbler of juice to her mouth. A dribble escaped from one side as she drank. She was delicate, a little bird. Katie was the strong one - always climbing things, eating more, gulping juice. Always brave. Present.

The toast popped up and I grabbed it quickly, buttered it generously, sliced it, dropped it onto Katie's plate.

'Mmmm...' I picked up a slice, took a bite with a show of great drama, before dropping it back onto the dish. I smiled to show that Katie and I were in cahoots, were the lucky ones.

'Now, don't go stealing that from Katie, Cara. You said you didn't want any,' and I winked in Katie's direction.

Cara frowned but said nothing.

We settled into silence. I enjoyed it, wallowed in it, and closed my eyes, as the light around us rose up slowly, steadily, into a white blue.

– – –

James hated Katie being around, and made this very clear on an almost daily basis.

'Surely her family miss her, Cara. She can't be with us every day,' he muttered.

'She's older than me,' Cara stated. 'She's nearly thirteen.'

'Thirteen or thirty, she must have her own home to go to,' he said, flatly, staring at his dinner while he loaded his fork with peas.

'Sshh!' Cara whined, 'She'll HEAR YOU!'

'She's in the bathroom,' I said.

James shot me a glance.

'I can say what I want in my own house,' he asserted, 'and what I want, is to be able to eat my dinner without having a strange girl sat at the table every night. A strange, silent girl. It's like sharing the table with a ghost,'

91

Nobody said anything more, and the room fell quiet. James was angry, brooding, and Cara hurt, scared of losing her friend, as she was each time he mentioned it. She was a lonely, fearful child at times, it struck me. I could see it in her eyes, the desperation that this might be it, this might be the day he sent Katie away; they flicked around the room, darting, following a sea of starlings, following a train of thought. Flitting.

I had to look away, she made me dizzy.

I knew what that feeling was like, to be terrified of losing someone.

Nausea sat at the pit of my stomach. I was back in that place, inside that small space. It was closing in. We stayed silent, and I concentrated on my food until I couldn't bear the sound of chewing and scraping any longer; I couldn't cope with the mastication, the saliva, and the teeth. I pushed back my chair suddenly, and stood up. James looked up, startled.

The kitchen door creaked gently open, as it often did, the room elbowing its way open, shouldering itself ajar. It was a temporary relief. The space opened up again.

'Where are you going?' he asked, surprised.

'To the bathroom,' I said.

'To see Katie?' Cara asked, with hope.

I looked at James.

'To see Katie,' I stated, just a little too loudly.

— — —

When James came home from work the next day, he found Cara at the table, drawing some sort of map, for homework. She bent close to the picture and her long, brown hair fell down around her face and across her neck.

The dishwasher hummed, the washing machine vibrated, the oven was on; the room was filled with the many voices of domesticity. They spoke to me. They calmed me.

'No Katie today?' he whispered into my ear, as he bent to kiss my cheek.

'She was here earlier,' I mouthed in reply.

James looked at the table.

'I'm laying dinner for three,' he said, 'barricade the front door,' he smiled, warmly; happy, so happy that it was just the three of us.

I didn't feel the same; felt guilty that I didn't.

I stirred the stroganoff, took in the rich scent and allowed my mind to wander until it filled the room, floated around the room, with the smell and the chatter of the house.

Katie was many things that Cara was not. Willing to try something new. Steady, never angry or emotional. She was constant, placid, yet strong. She was cold and solid, glacial in her self-confidence and yet warm in her humour. Often, Cara giggled beside her, happy for once, giddy and afloat with joy.

She might be with us too much, she might be a quiet, insidious presence, but she was a good one. And a good influence, I felt.

With a jolt, I realised I missed her when she was gone.

— — —

It was late, and James had been up in Cara's bedroom for over an hour. I heard the creak of her bedroom door, and the kitchen door swung in unison with it.

He was slightly red in the face when he came into the room, not making eye contact.

'I need a beer,' he stated.

'What happened?' I asked, quietly, as I opened the fridge. The harsh neon light came as a slither of cold into the room.

'The girl,' he said, 'that girl is nuts,'

'Who?' I asked, without thinking.

I passed him the beer.

'Who?' he asked, exacerbated, 'are you serious? Our bloody daughter.'

'Oh,' was all I could think to reply. I looked to my toes. And then, 'why exactly?'

'We need to get her to stop. She can't spend the rest of her life seeing ghosts, or imaginary people, or whatever the hell it is; I just told her. She's not real. You're just imagining it. I was nice, of course I was nice, but I told her the truth. A few home truths.'

'Oh, James,' I sighed, 'she isn't crying, is she?'

'It'll do her good in the end,' he stated.

I walked out the kitchen and up the stairs.

– – –

It was 5 a.m. and I crept out of the bedroom, down the stairs.

My mind was full of thoughts, hovering thoughts, migrating from memory to present. They were filling my head, filling my brain and spinning, gliding, circling each other. There were too many there. Too many words, concepts, pictures.

I wondered if I would go mad.

I pushed the kitchen door further ajar and stepped through. The room was indigo, and through the window above the sink I could see the sky: cobalt, with a shattered patch of pink.

I poured myself a glass of water. Tried to focus on the view. My heart was racing in my chest; an old feeling, a terrifying one.

Fear.

It had become a memory, I realised, this fear. It was a memory that had settled in the back of my mind, ever present. It was a nest. But what James had said, everything that was happening, had awoken it. I had thought I was moving on, and over it, but I wasn't. All I had been doing was allowing it to sit comfortably.

And grow.

Because the fact of the matter was this: there should be two children sat my table. There should be. But there was only one.

– – –

The next morning, I woke late. I woke to the sound of a blackbird, unexpectedly close to the house, singing for pure joy.

Downstairs, James and Cara were talking, eating breakfast. I could hear him placing dirty dishes in the sink as she chattered gently. I put on my dressing gown and went down to see them. James turned at the sound of me entering the room, nodded towards Cara at the table.

'Someone's had two pieces of toast,' he said. 'All to themselves,' he added, pointedly.

He grinned.

'Mummy,' Cara said, 'we let you have a lie in,'

'I can see that, darling. Thank you.'

'We're off to school now, aren't we Cazza? Go and get your shoes on, there's a good girl,' James said, touching the top of her head, so delicately. With such love.

Cara got up and skipped out the room.

'She'll be OK,' he stated.

'I know she will,' I said.

James leant forward and kissed me on the cheek again, then walked past me into the hall, to the sound of Cara struggling with her shoelaces, muttering to herself. I listened to them for a brief moment, caught still in the space of my eavesdropping. Enjoying their intimacy. Until they both called out to me, wished me goodbye, and I heard the front door slam.

It was so very soft. It was so very still.

I stood for a moment, suddenly awash with sadness, blue. I gripped the edge of the kitchen table. I was on a precipice, almost falling. I was holding on with the tips of my fingers, unsure why. Unsure whether to simply let go. I could let go.

The kitchen door groaned gently ajar again. I watched it as it crept into the room, changing the space, and the light. Changing the air.

I took a deep breath.

'Now Katie,' I said, 'would you like some toast?'

Acknowledgements

Thank you to all my friends and family for their ongoing encouragement and support: especially Mandy, Sarah and Carol, whose faith in me exceeds my own, but has spurred me to keep on writing.

I am indebted to my writer friends, Julie, Patrick and Roger, who have all given freely of their time and opinions, although none of them had heard from me for some time prior to my unsolicited communications asking for their thoughts. Not only talented, clearly, they are also nice people, with generous souls.

Special thanks to my beta-readers, Julia and Stuart, whose invaluable feedback has ensured, I hope, that these stories don't only make sense in my head but on the page as well. You have both given me hours of your time, and I appreciate it greatly.